ONE
FORBIDDEN
KNIGHT

ONE FORBIDDEN KNIGHT

NICOLA DAVIDSON

Entangled Publishing, LLC
2614 South Timberline Road
Suite 109
Fort Collins, CO 80525
Visit our website at www.entangledpublishing.com.

Scandalous is an imprint of Entangled Publishing, LLC.

Edited by Kate Brauning
Cover Design by Syd Gill
Cover Art by The Killion Group, Inc.

ISBN 978-1-943892-89-1

Manufactured in the United States of America

First Edition October 2015

Scandalous
an Entangled imprint

For my all-round amazing CP and friend Sherilee Gray—
I'm so lucky to have you in my life. And for three fabulous
little ladies/future heroines: Madison, Sasha, and Tahlia, with
much love.

Chapter One

She was late. Horribly, fearfully, catastrophically late.
Gritting her teeth against a wave of self-directed anger,
Catherine Linwood hurried down a wide, icy-cold corridor
within St. James's Palace as fast as she could without hitching
up her dark blue damask skirts and sprinting.

So few people had the trust and affection of their gracious
and beloved sovereign Queen Mary. As the only child of Her
Majesty's most favored physician, Arthur Linwood, she had
been warmly welcomed to court, granted countless audiences,
and given gifts and elegantly furnished rooms.

Now she was repaying the kindnesses with tardiness.

"Catherine, please…" a voice wheezed beside her, and she
glanced at Lady Jane Howard, whose complexion currently
matched her plum-colored gown. Reluctantly, she slowed her
steps.

"I'm sorry, Jane. We are a quarter hour late. You know how Her Majesty feels about punctuality."

"Yes, but we'll hardly impress dripping perspiration and gasping like landed trout. Besides, it was feast preparations for your father's return, not dallying with a gentleman. It was her ladies and their winter ills that kept him away in the country so long."

Catherine nodded, but her anxiety didn't ease. Papa would be furious if he knew she'd kept the queen waiting, especially in her current delicate state.

"I couldn't bear to distress her. She is so close to term now. Just think, finally England and Spain will be joined together again. It feels like we've waited forever for a Catholic prince, especially after the last mishap. Poor, dear lady. All the signs, but no bab—"

"Hush!" her friend hissed.

"It's true."

Abruptly, Jane grabbed her elbow in an unrelenting grip and yanked her well away from the courtiers calling out greetings and bowing as they passed. "Don't be a fool. True or false, it is dangerous to speak of such things. It always travels back, and then you're arrested and made a head shorter. A person's name, friends, whether they are even guilty, none of that matters. You're a favorite one day and decorating London Bridge the next."

Catherine winced. No one knew better than a Howard how precarious the love of a monarch could be. Old King Henry had executed Jane's father the Earl of Surrey, and her cousins Katherine Howard and Anne and George Boleyn.

"You're right. I won't—"

"Good. Just pray for the queen and her unborn child. As

long as Elizabeth is heir, there'll be plots and rebellion. That sly red fox should be rotting in the Tower. Her mother tore this country apart, and she would too."

"But she's your *cousin*," Catherine mumbled, suppressing a twinge of sympathy at the rough treatment the queen's half-sister had endured over the years. "Distant cousin," said Jane coldly. "And a heretic, no matter what she claims. All proper, God-fearing people shun and despise her. You are a devoted Catholic, aren't you Catherine?"

"Of course!"

"Good. If Elizabeth were to become queen, the country would never recover. Look at the turmoil when Edward was king, then that usurper Jane Grey. Protestants make terrible rulers. They are weak and ungodly."

"Papa says—"

"Bah. Your father should do naught but doctor. And find you a husband while he has influence and you have your looks. Men might overlook a small dowry and lack of title now, even that you've studied Latin texts and tended uncovered limbs. But you are twenty years old, and time is swiftly running out."

Guilt prickled, the kind that warranted a confessional visit. Disloyalty to her beloved father was wrong, but her lack of husband had become a matter of embarrassment. Papa always laughed and said the day a worthy man presented himself—a kind, devout, and sober Catholic who treated his servants well—he would heartily consent. When she'd seen the unsuccessful men stomp away, with their sour breath and padded doublets, she'd been glad of the firm edict. But lately, she wasn't so certain.

"Perhaps I shall be a merry old maid, dancing till dawn

and eating sweetmeats all day," Catherine said eventually, forcing a cheerful grin. "You may visit when your castles, jewels, and future lordly husband grow tiresome."

"Ha! And you may always visit me. Even if we must roll you from room to room and winch you upstairs. Now, let's see to Her Majesty."

Relieved at her friend's restored humor, they swiftly rounded the last corner of the torch-lit stone corridor and halted outside a pair of wide oak doors blocked by two heavily armed guards.

Taking a deep breath, Catherine smoothed the front of her gown and patted her head to ensure her wayward ebony curls were still secured under a modest velvet hood. It was ridiculous to be nervous, but usually her father stood beside her, and without his calm, black-gowned presence, that comforting scent of herbs and fresh linen, she felt a touch alone. It was always so hard when he was away tending others. Their rooms felt too big without his chatter, his husky laugh, the bubbling of boiling water and knocking of pestle and mortar as he tried new elixir recipes.

Before she could say a word, Jane glared at the guards.

"Do you not know who we are? Let us pass at once!"

"Yes, Lady Jane. Mistress Catherine," said one of the guards quickly, bowing respectfully as he immediately turned to knock on the door.

Eventually one of Queen Mary's ladies appeared to usher them both through. As she followed the two other women into a short passageway, Catherine turned her head and smiled apologetically at the man. As much as she loved Jane, no guard or servant ever moved fast enough for her friend. When the Howards were in power, they more than made up for the times they weren't.

In the queen's spacious chamber, her nose wrinkled at the strong odor of perspiration, tallow and perfume. As was custom for childbed seclusion, there was a large fire for heat and candles for light as the windows were boarded over to stop ill winds. It made the area almost unbearably stuffy and taxing for the ladies who attended Her Majesty constantly. Several sat embroidering, one strummed a harp and three more played cards, but all looked flushed and uncomfortable.

"Are you all right now? Do you need me?"

Catherine grinned at the look of sheer longing Jane directed toward the card game. "Go. Go and unburden those poor women of their coins."

"If you're sure…" her friend replied, but she had already half-crossed the room.

"Catherine," boomed a deep, almost manly voice.

She spun around and sank into a low curtsy as Queen Mary ambled toward her, a flowing ermine-trimmed cream gown brushing the floor with each of the petite monarch's steps.

"Your Majesty. I beg your forgiveness for my lateness today."

"We shall excuse you today, child, but do not keep us waiting again when we have need of you."

"No, madam. Never. Are you well?"

"As can be expected," the queen replied, resting a bejeweled hand on her hugely distended belly. "But everyone will rest better once the child is born. Our seclusion is just begun, yet already we are weary of these four walls. Perhaps you will join us in beseeching the Blessed Virgin for a swift and safe delivery?"

Catherine nodded eagerly. England desperately needed this child to secure the Catholic throne. Three years ago the queen and all those around her had thought her to be pregnant, but there had never been a babe in her belly. This time was different. And Papa, the greatest physician in all of England, would have the honor of delivering the heir.

"Madam, you are in my daily prayers. And King Phillip of course. I hope...I hope very much he will be able to return to England soon."

Mary sighed, her expression unbearably sad. "That is our dearest wish, but Spanish affairs of state keep him most occupied. He is the best of rulers, so just and dutiful."

"Of course."

"Come here and tell us your news," the queen said, carefully settling herself into a cushioned throne and beckoning Catherine over to a footstool. "It will be a pleasant diversion."

"Shall I rub your feet for you?"

"Sweet child. So like your mother, God rest her soul. I wish..."

Glancing up from carefully removing the queen's shoes, Catherine almost shivered at the truly odd expression on Mary's face. Hard. Calculating. And yet sorrowful too.

"Yes, madam?"

"All wrongs will be made right once our son is born. We ask you to remember that. And know as an obedient and faithful subject, we shall always hold you fondly in our heart."

"How could I not be?" she said carefully, confused at the queen's intense words. "The prince will make England whole again. We'll all rejoice."

Just for a moment, Mary looked away, one hand clutching

the strand of polished rosary beads about her neck. Then she turned back, smiling.

"Indeed. And once we are recovered, we will hold a feast, and you shall be introduced to some fine gentleman. Past time you were married…unless our Lord is now calling you to a different purpose?"

Catherine paused in her gentle rubbing of the queen's swollen right foot. "No, madam. I still hope to marry. Very much. A special man, handsome, learned and charming would be most agreeable."

The queen chuckled, a hint of color brightening her usually pale cheeks and livening her brown eyes. "A list! My word. Should he be a lord? A knight? A physician?"

"Well, I…"

"Let me pass! Your Majesty! Your Majesty!"

Catherine jumped at the hoarse cry, but Mary remained very still, calmly watching her personal page's stumbling approach.

"Yes, boy?"

"Majesty, I bring grave news."

"Then do not tarry, tell me."

"It's Doctor Linwood, Majesty. He's—"

"What?" said Catherine sharply, all manners forgotten as icy fright crept down her spine and turned her hands clammy. Had her father caught the fever he'd gone to tend? Fallen from his horse?

The page inclined his head, his eyes somber. "Mistress, I am grieved to report Doctor Linwood has passed away."

Catherine stared uncomprehendingly. No. Passed away meant dead. And her father was hale, hearty, and shortly to be dining with her. Turbot, roasted beef, marzipan fruit, and a good wine to celebrate his homecoming.

"Don't be ridiculous," she said, pushing the words out past the driest tongue in Christendom. "I received a message earlier, he returns this evening. You must be mistaken."

His gaze didn't waver. "No, mistress. I'm so sorry. It was his weak heart. And ill humors from traveling in the rain."

"Papa never travels in the rain. And he certainly didn't have a weak heart!"

"Are you sure? I—"

"Thank you," snapped Queen Mary. "That will be all."

The page immediately bowed low and hurried away, but Catherine barely noticed. Shocking, crushing cold enveloped her, making her body shake and vision gray.

Dead.

Sounds erupted. An awful high, keening wail like a soul condemned to purgatory. Women shouting and heavy boots crossing the stone floor. Chairs scraping and steel flashing. Clamping her hands over her ears, she fought to escape the noise, awkwardly falling from her stool and huddling in a ball.

Dead.

Without warning, impersonal arms hauled her to her feet and a pungent blend of lavender and vinegar assailed her nose. The world spun and spun, and she coughed and clawed at the arms, desperate for an anchor, some way to halt the terror advancing on her like a relentless French army.

The scent came again, choking, overwhelming, but finally relief, as she fell into blessed darkness.

Everything about the day screamed death. From the unnatural slate-gray sky and bone-chilling wind to the dull, ponderous rhythm of the church bells confirming another soul's departure.

Sir Brandon FitzAlan pulled a flagon of wine from a hidden pocket in his thick black cloak and took several healthy gulps. He was entirely too sober for this and his damned servants were to blame for his rare state of total awareness. Instead of wine, he'd been presented with watered ale all day. One particularly hardy soul, a fourth generation maid with the temperament of a bear woken during hibernation, had actually set a goblet of warmed milk in front of him at breakfast.

Milk.

His stomach lurched, and he coughed, pulled the cloak closer about him, and strode forward past several clusters of gray-and-black-clad mourners who wished to pay their respects but weren't familiar enough to the family to enter the crypt. As always, he ignored the curious stares, the whispers, the deferential curtsies and bows from those who feared or respected his very powerful family.

God's blood, he was weary of death. Not only that, he was disgusted by the ugly, hollow shell England had become under the rule of Bloody Mary Tudor—the beheadings and burnings all in the name of her cursed religion. If this woman had her way, England would be naught more than Spanish territory, dragged back to the dark ages and ruined. She'd even managed to lose the jewel of Calais back to the French;

Old Henry would be turning in his grave.

Some called the queen generous. Indeed, so generous she'd sent Arthur Linwood, the finest man he'd ever known, the doctor who'd saved his mother's life, into the heart of a small plague outbreak. Robbing England of one of its most gifted physicians. Robbing a child of a beloved father.

Damn her to hell.

Finally reaching the Linwood family crypt, he dropped to one knee and bowed his head. His hose was no match for the cold, damp stone but the discomfort was naught compared to grief and rage. His friend and savior was dead.

"Why?" Brand burst out, anger almost robbing him of breath. "I don't understand. Why you, Arthur?"

"I don't understand either."

His head jerked up at the soft, tear-soaked voice. He hadn't even seen the woman sitting in a shadowed corner, dressed in a heavy and rather shapeless black velvet gown, with a modest black hood and thick lace veil covering her face. Yet the pure misery in her tone reflected his. She wasn't a casual acquaintance or a courtier attending to see and be seen. This woman had truly adored Arthur Linwood.

"Forgive me, madam," he said, inclining his head. "I didn't mean to intrude."

"You aren't," she replied, standing and pushing the veil back from her face.

Brand sucked in a harsh breath at the perfection revealed—thickly lashed, deep blue eyes set in a pale oval face with a slightly pointed nose, high cheekbones, and full, pink lips, all framed by pitch-black curls. Had such a beauty been Arthur's lover? His friend's wife had long passed, no doubt the man would have been lonely with only a young daughter for company. If so, he'd been remarkably discreet. In their country jaunts, their many alehouse meetings, Arthur had never mentioned a woman, only his pride and joy: clever, amusing little Carey. Perhaps she was Carey's nurse? Her aunt or older cousin? In which case he could leave with a clear conscience. Even in her terrible grief, she had an air of quiet gentleness that spoke of a kind and loving guardian to a child.

"Sir?" she said, briefly resting her hand on his. "Are you well?"

He frowned at her concern, unnerved by something rarely shown to him as much as the heated jolt from her light, innocent touch. He clearly needed to find himself a lusty wench and a great deal of wine. Tonight. Yet first he had to pose the question.

"Well enough," Brand said, clearing his throat. "I don't mean to be indelicate, but by chance are you a relative? Perhaps little Carey's nurse? Arthur was a dear friend, and I should like to know his daughter will be well cared for, and to offer funds if needed."

"It is very kind of you to care about my well-being, but I'm not so little."

He froze. "What? You can't be Carey! She's a girl, not, er…"

Unexpectedly, she smiled, a ray of sunshine in the cold, gloomy crypt.

"It is Catherine Mary actually, but I never could pronounce it as a child. I'm not sure why Papa would speak of me as if I were still young. I'm twenty."

Brand stiffened. He could guess. What loving father would want a heretic, a nobleman's wretched bastard, lusting after his beautiful, pure, Catholic daughter?

"I've heard a lot about you," he said gruffly. "Apart from your age, of course. I am Sir Brandon FitzAlan."

Her eyes widened.

"Then my father misled us both. For when he spoke of his friend Brand, I thought he meant…"

A reluctant chuckle rumbled in his chest as several emotions chased each other across her expressive features. "An old man? I am. A few months shy of thirty summers."

Catherine's cheeks took on a rosy hue. "Someone closer to his own age. And status. He never mentioned the title, and I don't think I've seen you at court. Are you…?"

"I'm rarely in London, but yes, I'm one of those FitzAlans. The current Earl of Arundel is my fa…first cousin," he finished hastily, shocked he'd nearly blurted the long-hidden truth. *What the hell was wrong with him?* "I never bothered using my title with Arthur. Three years ago he saved my mother's life, quite frankly he could have called me whatever he pleased. But it was always Brand, and I gladly called him friend."

"A death does tend to reveal true friends."

His jaw clenched. How well a widower knew that particular truth. Doubly so when the death was most untimely and raised more questions than answers, when finger-pointing and rumors reached feverish levels. He'd already been on a dark path. If his mother had died he no doubt would have succumbed entirely to the black devils in his soul.

"Indeed it does," he replied with a curt nod. "How do you find your friends at this time?"

"Her Majesty is wonderful. I often attend her in her rooms, but she hasn't been feeling well the past few days, so instead sent notes. And I know the local poor have benefitted enormously from her bountiful alms in my father's name."

"But what of you?"

"I…"

Catherine's lush lips curved in a fond smile, and again he fought a heightened awareness, the strong desire to trace her mouth with his thumb. Or tongue.

"Yes?"

"I am most fortunate. She is always so kind to me. I shall keep our rooms at the palace until I marry. Half again my dowry. And some damask and linen, too."

"Very generous," he said evenly, barely managing to mask his disgust at the pitiful offering. How fast they forgot a life of highly-skilled and loyal service. In this regard Queen Mary was certainly her father's daughter.

"It is generous," Catherine said sharply, staring at the stone floor. "I am most grateful for her compassion in allowing me to remain in the palace. I have no other family, no pending marriage, nowhere else to go. Papa and I…we never had our own home, always loaned rooms. And I don't think I could bear to be parted from his belongings. The books and that scent of crushed h-herbs he always h-had…"

"I know it," he said quickly, soothingly. "I don't think anyone in England bathed as much as your father. Often suspected he was part fish. A well-seasoned fish, naturally. Thyme, a little parsley…"

Her head shot up, and she stared hard at him, her lips trembling. "P-parsley?"

Brand sighed. Clearly he should not be permitted near anyone while sober.

"You're right. T'was a far more manly scent. Er…basil?"

"Mint," said Catherine in an odd, suffocated voice, and suddenly she hurled herself against his chest and wept, silent, wrenching sobs that shook her entire frame.

Instinctively, his arms closed around her. His second mistake, after making conversation without the benefit of sufficient wine, for it was immediately apparent Arthur's precious daughter was a grown woman. Lusciously so. This close, not even a shapeless gown could disguise her full and firm breasts, slender waist, and generous hips.

"There now, don't cry," he said uneasily, awkwardly patting her shoulder while attempting to put distance between them before his unruly body responded to her warm, soft curves in an altogether inappropriate way. Besides, these were real tears. What did he know of genuine, heartfelt emotion from a young woman?

Damnation. They were in a crypt. She was the virginal daughter of his deceased friend, a favorite of the wretched Queen of England, and a damned Catholic.

What in the hell was he doing?

What in the name of the saints was she doing, standing in a cold crypt and weeping in the arms of a stranger?

Yet it felt so good, if entirely different.

Sir Brandon was the physical opposite of her father—so tall her forehead barely reached his collarbone, with wide, wide shoulders and a huge chest that stretched taut a beautifully embroidered dark green doublet. A heavy gold chain announced his wealth and position, as did the fur-trimmed cloak caressing her cheek. As for the heavily muscled arms wrapped around her, oddly, she'd never felt so safe. He might be a man she knew of only through Papa's mentions, but surely anyone her father befriended would only be good and honorable.

Finally, her tears slowed to a trickle, and he gently set her away from him and stepped back. She immediately missed his warmth, but it did permit a better view of his face.

Perhaps the most interesting face she'd ever seen. Not handsome in a traditional sense; his hair too brown, clean shaven jaw too square, cheekbones too harsh and nose slightly too big to be celebrated by court artists. But they would never quite capture him on canvas. Not the golden shade of his skin or emerald-green of his eyes, so startling under slashing dark brown brows. Definitely not those firm lips which probably fuelled the secret kissing fantasies of every woman from here to York.

"Is there a spot on my face?"

Catherine jumped at the amused question, her cheeks burning. "Ah...no. No, Sir Brandon. I was just looking at your...eyes. Such an unusual color. Lovely."

He tilted his head, those lips twitching. "It's just Brand. And the eyes are courtesy of my mother's Scottish ancestors, I believe."

"Scottish?"

"Don't look so horrified. It was no doubt a border raid. Celtic lasses can be rather single-minded and Englishmen not overly resistant to temptation. Now, you must forgive me my short stay, but I have a meeting I must away to. Again may I say how sorry I am for your loss, and should you ever need anything, be assured I am at your service."

"Thank you," she replied dully, her heart sinking like a stone in a millpond at his abrupt eagerness to leave. Impersonal coolness now replaced the smile, and no wonder. She'd hurled herself at him like a tipsy chambermaid, babbled about his eyes and offended him. Brand was a powerful nobleman, one of the great FitzAlans. Catherine Linwood a poor nobody, an orphan. Their only connection was a dead man.

He bowed and turned to leave her life forever.

"Wait, B-Brand," she burst out, unable to bear the thought of losing a man both closely linked to her father, and the first to make her heart skip a beat. "There is something. A service, I mean."

"Yes?"

"I would know how my father died."

He frowned. "They did not tell you? I assumed given where he was, he had fallen victim to the plague."

Frustration and uncertainty rose in her belly, a sensation undiminished since she'd awoken in her father's rooms and remembered the brief and rather vague explanation of his death. She was a learned doctor's daughter, not some silly noblewoman who even feared bathing.

"No. The other court doctors said nothing of the plague. Although his body was prepared and buried immediately, they returned his satchel, boots, cap, and crucifix to me."

A long pause stretched to eternity.

"What exactly were you told, Catherine?" he said finally, his face impassive, but his green eyes were stormy and massive shoulders taut with tension.

"That he died of a weak heart, and a sudden onset of ill humors after being caught outside in heavy rains and mud. But, Brand, his health was always excellent. And he never traveled in poor weather. Ever. Papa always told me to expect him a day or two later because riding in the rain is bad for the chest and lungs, and he couldn't abide carriages."

"If the queen is due to deliver her child shortly, he would have made all haste to return to the palace. Perhaps he didn't wish to worry you with a health matter."

A sudden bone-deep weariness made her shoulders sag. "Perhaps. No, you're right. I am being fanciful. Forgive me, it has been—"

"I'll find out," Brand said roughly. "He was my friend, and I'd not have you distressed. Just give me a week or so."

Before she could reply, he bowed low and strode from the crypt, taking his warmth and strength away.

Rubbing her arms, Catherine shivered. With one last glance around the oppressive, confined space, she hitched up her gown and hurried out into the damp London air, over to where a bored guard sat perched on a rock between a row of grave markers.

The man got to his feet, a look of relief on his ruddy face.

"Ready to return to the palace, Mistress?"

"Yes, thank you."

Brand would visit soon. She had one thing to look forward to, at least.

Chapter Two

If there was one thing he couldn't abide, it was a mystery. Resting one elbow on a solid wooden ledge, Brand stared hard out a diamond-paned library window of his London home to where the gray, choppy Thames was doing its best to offer the passengers of several barges an impromptu freezing bath. Exactly what he felt like doing to several suddenly discreet citizens. Discovering the details of Arthur Linwood's passing should have been an easy task, yet he'd hit a stone wall of pale-faced silence at every turn. Nonplussed, he'd sent out several of his own men to see what they could unearth. Because he didn't trust the queen as far as the belly in front of her, he'd also instructed another to keep a discreet eye on Catherine and report even the slightest suspicious behavior towards her. Lucas was a loyal lad, even if he was a talkative troublemaker and possessing a fourteen year old's unique ability to demolish thrice his weight in food. He just couldn't watch over her himself. Catherine was too young. Too vulnerable. Too open. Too beautiful. Too damned everything. A base, wine-soaked heretic like him would be poison to an innocent like her, yet he'd been unable to banish the woman from his mind. Clearly, the sooner this odd matter was resolved, the better.

"God's blood, Brandon! You're not listening to me."

Masking his irritation, he turned and smiled pleasantly at Henry FitzAlan, 19th Earl of Arundel. The dark-eyed, older lord was about the most powerful in the kingdom, a devout Catholic and someone who never missed an opportunity to aggressively further his own interests. As evidenced with this particular one-sided conversation.

"Of course I'm listening to you, Father. You wish me to leave the agreeable and supremely peaceful existence of widower and re-enter the unholy state of matrimony. Unfortunately I have yet to hear from you a single good reason why."

Arundel scowled, an expression which did his overly prominent nose no favors.

"A request from me is reason enough. It's been four years. If you do not marry again, the rumors surrounding Therese's death will never abate. I am only thinking of your well-being. And that of your mother. Susanna must be very lonely in the country without the companionship of another highborn woman. I should insist she come to London and take her rightful place at court."

Brand somehow suppressed a laugh. His father could insist all he liked, but it would take several armies to remove his mother from their West Berkshire estate. She hated London and Arundel equally, and as his grandfather's passing had left her explicitly and generously provided for, the earl couldn't even bend her to his will through blackmail.

A fact which frustrated the man no end.

"As always, I will pass on your greetings and good wishes."

"Bah. Tis unnatural, her acceptance of your sinful and wayward existence."

Brand's fists clenched. "She understands I have no desire to wed again."

"You must. Despite past events—"

"My lord. Such a benign phrase for my wife taking her own life."

His father's gaze turned colder than a northern wind. "...*despite past events* there are still many noblewomen willing to accept your hand in marriage. You have a duty to your family to sire sons. A duty to God and country."

"My family?" he repeated softly, too angry to ignore the unspoken warning. "You mean those who ordered my mother to abort me? Who continuously threatened and harassed her during my childhood? Who to this day cling pathetically to the myths of your saintliness and us being *cousins*?"

Arundel thumped his empty pewter goblet down on a carved oak side table. "How many times must we have this out? I was a lad of sixteen, Brandon. Sixteen! There was no proof but her word...and my father had far different ambitions for me. But even if I cannot openly acknowledge our true relationship, I have done well for you, have I not? More than well."

Brand turned away. It was either that or pummel his father to the consistency of jellied eel. Unlike his devil relatives, the man had ruthlessly ignored his bastard son for twenty-five years, providing nothing and allowing no contact between his three children and their half-sibling. Then came 1553, a tumultuous year for Arundel including his release from imprisonment for suspected plotting, and the deaths of King Edward and Lady Jane Grey. Near-mortality had clearly bitten hard, as handwritten notes, coins, bolts of cloth and a thoroughbred stallion arrived for his cherished "cousin." A barrage of personal meetings, forced name change and a royal summons to court for a knighting ceremony followed, as did the swift marriage to Catholic heiress Lady Therese Fairfax after she was "discovered" naked in his palace accommodation.

Done well was highly debatable. Although there was one service Arundel had rendered that he would never forget: securing Arthur Linwood's gifted expertise.

"Indeed, sir," he said eventually, through teeth clenched so hard they would grind to powder. "Most well."

"Excellent. Then I shall look forward to seeing you at the feast next week to give thanks for our impending royal heir. Several fine young ladies will be present. Oh, and by the by, Brandon, it would also be prudent to attend Mass more publicly. Start your new life as you mean to go on."

"My lord."

Fortunately he was spared any further response as the five-foot, eight-inch and growing, black-haired whirlwind of chaos known as Lucas stumbled into the room with a tray full of cakes, fruit, and a meat pie. "Ohhh, beg pardon, milord."

"Master de Vere," replied Arundel with a tight-lipped smile as he strode past. "Cousin. Good day."

Lucas perched his gangly frame on the edge of a table. "Really don't know why he bothers with that cousin mummery. Truth is plain as the nose on both your faces. Old

Henry acknowledged his boy, why can't Arundel?"

"Your godfather also cropped people at the neck for speaking out of turn. By the saints, boy, your mouth is going to get you killed one day."

"They'd have to catch me first. Then fight me."

Brand sighed. This was Lucas's ninth noble household in two years for "education and advancement". He'd been deposited here by a visibly relieved Arundel three months previously. Allegedly the lad was ungodly and uncontrollable, endured solely because he was the old king's godchild and eldest son of a legendary warrior, then smilingly gifted on when sanity ran out. Personally, he found the boy intelligent and trustworthy, just easily bored and prone to blurt each and every thought he had.

"What are you doing back so early, Lucas? Something to report?"

The boy's brown eyes sharpened. "Actually surprised to find you here. Thought you'd be at the inn waiting for Mistress Linwood."

A chill slithered down his spine. "What inn?"

"Ack, you are getting old. Your message! Told her to meet you at the Grand Duke Inn over in Tewkesbury Lane. She left to go there with two guards so I thought all must be well and came back here for a late lunch…Sir Brand? What's wrong?"

A curse so foul left his lips that even Lucas blanched. Then he stalked to a cupboard, found the plainest cloak he possessed, an old black velvet cap left behind by a long ago drinking companion, and his sharpest dagger.

"Come with me," he snarled, shoving the dagger into a hidden pocket in the cloak while one thought pounded his head as relentlessly as a drumbeat.

Please be safe.

Her heart was beating so fast, her mind so awhirl, Catherine scarcely felt the uneven cobbled street under her shoes.

All might soon be better with the world. Brand had sent a personal messenger asking her to meet him at the Grand Duke, a busy, respectable inn she'd visited many times with her father. Finally, she would know the truth of his death and be able to sleep again at night. Finally, she could think of a possible future, instead of the darkness of losing the only family she had.

She smiled ruefully. And she would see Brand, of course. The time between their meeting in the crypt and now felt like years even though it had only been several days. This time she would behave like a grown woman and true lady— calm and gracious in a modest, properly fitting dark brown velvet gown and matching hood. Definitely no weeping over herbs or nonsense about his eyes or ancestry.

Not to mention it was truly a blessing to leave the lovely but stifling confines of St. James's Palace. Queen Mary was still unwell, Jane suddenly summoned to her brother's side to act as hostess for a feast of thanksgiving, and other friends surprisingly scarce, so she'd been terribly lonely.

"Flower for milady?"

Blinking, she glanced down at the small, raggedly dressed and shivering girl holding up a half-wilted lily.

Before she could reply, one of the two sour-faced guards

leading the way halted and turned. "Away, you. Don't be bothering the mistress or you'll feel the back of me hand."

The child shrank back, and Catherine shot an annoyed look at the guard before delving into her fur-trimmed cloak pocket for a copper she couldn't truly afford now. "I would love a flower, sweetheart. Isn't it pretty? Here, for your trouble."

"Cor, God bless ye, milady," the girl replied excitedly, bobbing a curtsey, and dashing away with her prize.

Lifting the white and orange-flecked bloom to her nose, she inhaled the fading scent of the lily. It was still delicious, a pleasant contrast to the aroma hanging heavily over the surrounding narrow houses, pie stalls, and various shops. There was no wind today, just a cool, bleak dampness that somehow made the smell of perspiring people, cooking fat, stagnant water, and something foul she didn't want to think about, so much worse.

"Milady! Milady!"

Catherine stifled a groan. Clearly word had spread quickly. "Yes?" she said, glancing to her right. Yet rather than a mob of other undersized flower sellers, a young man appeared and doffed his cap.

"Mistress Linwood," he whispered quickly, taking her arm so he could speak directly into her ear. "I beg ye, *run*. These men mean ye harm."

She froze. "Excuse me?"

"Please ma'am. I've been waiting for days. It's getting about the city, the questions about ye father's death, and they don't like it one bit."

Spinning on her heel so she stood between the two guards and the slender young man, she stared hard at his bearded face, searching for any signs of trickery. But his gaze was steady and open.

"Who are you?" she said urgently, the words barely forming through chattering teeth.

"I'm Robbie Blacksmith, from Guildford. But that don't matter. What does matter is that it weren't a fever. There was a fight. Bad one. Two men telling the doctor he was wrong, and if he knew what was good fer him he would shut his mouth. It were summin' about her ma—"

"Oi!" bellowed one of her guards. "Get away from the lady. Back, or you'll feel a sword to the gullet."

"No!" Catherine burst out. "He's fine. It is fine."

Both guards ignored her, and Robbie was torn away, his arms viciously jerked behind his back.

"Country scum," the second guard hissed. "Just you wait. Stocks and irons for you, me lad."

Robbie struggled hard in the brutal hold. "I saw. I SAW. Doctor Linwood didn't die of no illness. A knife. He was staaaaaaa…"

Time seemed to stall. One moment Robbie stood on the edge of the cobbled street, the next he flew awkwardly through the air and landed with a sickening thud in the middle of the thoroughfare, directly in the path of a heavily-laden cart.

She screamed a warning, but he didn't move, and the next sound she heard was the horrifying crunch and grind of wooden wheels shattering human bones.

Bile filled her mouth, and she choked it down. Yet even as a mass of yelling and screaming people pushed past her to stare at the bloody carnage in the street, only Robbie's fierce words echoed in her ear.

I beg ye. RUN.

Crossing herself and whispering a fervent prayer for his immortal soul, she glanced quickly around for the guards. Thanks to the relentless curiosity of Londoners, there were now at least ten people between her and them. Taking a shaky breath, forgetting every one of the edicts Papa had ever taught about ladylike behavior, she turned, shoving and elbowing her way through the rapidly gathering crowd to run in the direction of the Grand Duke Inn.

Brand was there, waiting for her. He would know what to do, how to make sense of the words she'd heard, the sickening scene she'd just witnessed.

Blindly, she stumbled along the street, pushing past washerwomen, children splashing in puddles, and a group of men huddled around a crate with cards and coins piled on top.

"Mistress Linwood!"

Even as she desperately wanted to ignore the call, her head twisted to see the guards attempting to barrel their way through the throngs of people behind her. Forcing her aching legs to continue forward, she sent another prayer heavenward when she finally saw the familiar high wooden sign of the Grand Duke dangling from a wrought iron hook in the distance.

"MISTRESS LINWOOD! STOP!"

Terror nearly robbed her of breath at the furious roar, but this time she didn't pause to see how far behind the guards were. The inn was near. So near. Thirty feet at most. If she could just make it inside without causing a stir, Brand would find and protect her.

Some instinct compelled her to slow to a brisk walk—no

lady burst into an inn scarlet-faced and panting—and she swiftly reached up to check her elegant velvet hood was still in place. There and secure. Thank heavens. If she looked like a criminal, she would be thrown straight back out on the street—

The thought vanished in a surge of icy panic as two steel-like arms closed around her body. One crossed her breasts, clamping both elbows to her sides and leaving her hands dangling helplessly, the other sliding up so a large palm could seal her mouth, rendering an instinctive cry for help into nothing more than a muffled squeak. Finally, she was spun around like she weighed no more than a feather, away from the relative safety of the open street and into a dark, fetid alley.

Sweet blessed virgin.

They'd caught her.

Knowing he had perhaps a second or two before Catherine's limp shock turned into complete destruction of his shins, Brand hauled her further into the alley. It was particularly awful, blocked from the weakened sun's rays, dank and heavy with the putrid scents of piss, vomit, and stale ale. But beggars could hardly be choosers, and it would be perfect for his hastily put together half-plan.

He and Lucas had sprinted all the way here. He'd sent the boy to turn the Grand Duke upside down while he searched the surrounding streets. If he were a man who believed in everyday miracles, he'd be giving thanks for idiot guards who yelled her name as they chased. That he'd managed to get to her before they did, before she entered the inn was a relief beyond words. He had the sickest feeling she might not have left the place alive.

Keeping one hand clamped firmly over her mouth while evading her flailing hands, he put his lips hard against her ear.

"It's Brand, Carey. Don't scream. No matter what you were told, I never sent a messenger asking you to meet me at that inn. Nod if you understand."

Catherine's head jerked, her hands falling to her sides.

"Now," he continued, "forgive me for what I'm about to do."

Moving faster than he ever had in his life, Brand yanked off her well-crafted and recognizable headpiece and cloak, putting her long curls in total disarray. Ignoring her gasp of shock, knowing he was about to do far worse, he tore at her thankfully nondescript brown gown until one sleeve hung limply from her shoulder and simple linen petticoats showed. Lastly, hoping beyond words that the slimy black substance at his feet was just mud, he smeared her hem and right cheek and hiking up her skirts, shoved her up against the alley wall.

"B-Brand," she choked out as she tried to twist away from him, her eyes huge blue pools of terror. "Stop. Please. W-What…"

"Kick off one shoe and wrap your legs around my waist," he said harshly, pulling his faded felt cap lower over his forehead. "And for the love of God, do not speak. Not one word."

Her hesitation stretched to eternity, yet finally she gave a tiny nod.

"I trust you."

He groaned, relief at her acquiescence warring with anger at her misplaced faith and a spark of something softer he didn't dare define.

Furious at his lapse, Brand cupped the back of her head and crushed her mouth under his. Exactly what he expected he didn't know, but after a long moment of frozen shock, her lips softened in submission, and he nearly groaned again. On another occasion he might have smiled at her complete inexperience—her lips were willing but pressed together as tightly as stone masonry. Gentling his action, he coaxed them apart until his tongue could flick their kiss-swollen ripeness.

Catherine gasped, one hand clenching and unclenching the collar of his doublet. He felt the moment she surrendered fully, when her mouth opened for his tongue and her body relaxed, allowing him close enough so her ample breasts were pressed hard against his chest and his rapidly hardening cock could grind against that sweet spot between her legs.

He cursed softly, fighting the urge to yank down his hose and bury himself to the hilt inside her tight heat. He should have had a woman when he had the chance, because any finesse had vanished. Arthur's daughter, an untried virgin, with her low whimpers and untutored responses, was making him harder than he'd ever been in his life and soon, so soon, those base desires his wife had hated and run from would take over and…

"Oi! You there!"

They both stilled and a violent shudder passed through her frame. Slowly, deliberately, he turned her head away so all a passerby might see was unkempt hair and a grime-streaked cheek.

Panting for breath, he met the cold-eyed gazes of two scarlet-clad guards. Not the pair who had been chasing Catherine, but two others now blocked the end of the alley.

God's blood. Word was spreading.

"Yessirs?" he slurred, elongating his vowels to pure London tavern.

"What is going on here, then?" one of the guards barked.

Brand cocked his head and blinked several times, as though the question required much thought.

"Just a little swordplay with the, er, wife, sir."

"Is that right. And you, *mistress*? You often commit such lewdness in public?"

Before Catherine could speak, Brand forced a hearty laugh. "Alas, sir, my sweetheart is mute. Tis a great thing in a wife. Prettiest duckies around, but none of the damned quacking."

The second guard coughed, his lips twitching, and exchanged a glance with his companion. "Well. Turn your mind away from the birds for a moment. We're looking for a lady—"

"A *lady*, sir? In an *alley*?"

"We were…informed…she was last seen in this area."

"Ye have me baffled. Who was seen?"

"Catherine Linwood. Daughter of Arthur Linwood. Some called him doctor, but he was no more than a devil of dark spells, lies, and butchering."

Catherine's fingernails clawed his poor quality cloak, her body shaking, and a trickle of perspiration trailed a slick, itchy path down the back of his neck. Quickly, like he merely wished to stretch, Brand rubbed his cheek against hers, and thankfully she stilled again.

"Ain't never heard of her. What did she do? Steal summin? Run away from 'er lord 'n' master?"

"No. Far worse. Treason against Her Majesty the Queen. Blasphemy and plots with evil intent. We are posting drawings of her with a reward for capture."

"Oh-ho! What kind of reward?" he said loudly to muffle Catherine's broken whimper, hoping to sound greedily curious rather than violently ill.

"Coins and ale aplenty for a wise man who loves God and his good queen."

"Ye know," Brand said slowly, rubbing his chin and further blocking Catherine's face, "Think I did see a lady run past just before, going toward the inn. Fancy shoes sound different on these cobbles. And her hair was covered in one of them foine things with a veil. Thought mebbe she be late for mass or a banquet or such."

The first guard's hand closed around his sword handle, and Brand froze. Had that been too much? But the man merely leaned over and spat on the ground. "Mass is where you should be. Confessing your sins and begging forgiveness of our merciful Lord. Same for your mute. If she were a good, Christian woman she wouldn't be cursed with such an unholy affliction. On your way afore I whip you both bloody."

His heart sank at the one order that could reveal their deception, but obediently, he stepped backwards until Catherine's legs slid to the ground. Curling one arm around her shoulders, but under her dark, untidy curls, he held her seemingly loosely against his chest and silently urged his feet forward. Ten paces to temporary freedom. They could do this.

"Aye, sir. To church," he said, hunching his shoulders and staggering deliberately through a small mound of something revolting.

Both guards stepped back, unwilling to be soiled.

Five paces.

Forcing himself to amble, he nodded and continued, "Good day to ye."

The air outside the alley was the freshest he'd ever tasted, but still he hardly dared to breathe.

Stay hunched. Walk slowly. Keep Catherine upright.

With such a reward offered and more and more men joining the search, in a matter of hours, a day or two at best, Arthur's daughter would be the most hunted woman in England. Something damned ugly was going on, and it seemed to be connected to his friend's sudden passing. If he stayed with Catherine, he'd soon be seen and become a known accomplice.

Brand almost chuckled at the absurd thought, as if the decision hadn't already been made. Hell, he'd made himself Catherine's champion back in the crypt when he agreed to discover more about Arthur's death. It was probably his own inquiries that triggered the queen's wrath.

He cursed softly. For a man who knew more than most about the cruel lengths highborn people would go to in preserving their secrets, he'd been a bloody damned fool.

Now there could be only two options.

Flee.

Or die.

Chapter Three

The lane was quiet. So astonishingly quiet, the pounding of her heart sounded like the beat of a thousand drums.

Any moment there would be shouts, the fast thud of booted feet and the rasp of swords as they were unsheathed. Any moment she would be the one flying through the air then crumpled in a broken heap.

"Catherine?"

It sounded like Brand's baritone voice, but so far away. And muffled, like he sat underwater, although that was probably because one side of her face was crushed so hard against his chest she would have a doublet button imprint in her temple forever. Not to mention the haystack of curls covering her other ear and impairing her vision.

Yet she had no inclination whatsoever to move her head. Or any part of her limp body really. Brand was practically carrying her along the street under one arm, his strides long, purposeful, but unhurried. Numbness had left her useless, even the effort of breathing and keeping her eyes open a supreme one.

She'd thought the day her father died would be the worst of her life. But witnessing Robbie's accident, being chased by soldiers, hearing the terrible falsehoods about Papa…and how could it possibly be the worst and the best? She'd heard tales from indiscreet ladies at court, even witnessed the odd heated embrace. But nothing, nothing in the world could have prepared her for the searing reality of Brand's lips, his huge, hard chest pressing tightly against hers.

"*Catherine.*"

Brand again, this time louder and slightly impatient. She blinked and shook her head, anything to clear the fog in her mind. "You called me Carey before."

Almost imperceptibly, his stride faltered. "I had to. So you would know it was me and not someone else pretending to be a friend."

"Oh."

"Are you cold?"

"N-no," she replied through chattering teeth, her body abruptly wracked with shivers. The oddest sensation, especially when perspiration trickled down her upper arms and back. Unfortunately her wits were returning in a flood, and the cloying smell of sweat and whatever Brand had rubbed on her cheek and hem, the sight of her torn gown, and dirty cold-reddened bare feet made her want to vomit.

Brand sighed, pausing to remove his cloak, drape it around her shoulders then scoop her into his arms. He felt so warm, and once again so safe, she burrowed against him, curling one arm tightly around his shoulder and tucking her head against his neck.

"Just hold on," he said quietly. "We'll be home soon."

She jerked. "No, please! D-don't take me b-back to the palace. Those soldiers!"

"You aren't going back to that damned viper's nest. I'm taking you to my home until I work out what to do next."

"Not giving me up for c-coins and ale?" she said softly, a warmth seeping through her body that had nothing to do with his secure hold. Not only had he saved her from those wretched soldiers, he risked his own neck to offer a temporary sanctuary.

"As it happens, I have coins aplenty. And ale gives me a bellyache. Terribly unhealthy beverage, though not quite as bad as milk."

It might have been a joke, but something about his gruff tone made her relax and let out a long breath.

"I was so scared," she said slowly, trying to unravel her jumbled thoughts. "I don't understand any of this, Brand. The soldiers wanting to hurt me…those sinful lies about Papa. There is no way the queen would order this. Mary is a wonderful, kind, and generous woman who loves me as she loved my mother!"

There was a long, long silence. Then his grip tightened. "Tell me exactly what happened. Right from the beginning, when you got the message to meet me at the Grand Duke. Who told you to do that?"

"The queen's personal page. The same lad who told me of Papa's death when I was visiting Mary in her rooms. He had two guards with him, and said I had to leave right away as you were waiting for me at the inn. I know that place well. Papa and I often stopped there for food."

Brand cursed under his breath. "It was my fault, then.

Too damned indiscreet. I'm a bloody FitzAlan, someone is always watching."

She flinched at the harsh, bitter words. "Brand? What are you talking about?"

"Nothing. Just rambling," he said, the tip of one finger brushing her cheek in a soothing caress. "Go on. You walked from the palace?"

"Yes. The sun was out and I wanted to get some air. The guards agreed. All was well until we reached the corner of Tewkesbury Lane."

"Then what?"

Catherine shuddered as memories made her stomach roil.

"A little girl gave me a flower, and I paid her a coin. Then a young man appeared. He said…"

Her fingers bit into his shoulder as she again fought the urge to be horribly ill.

"Do you want me to stop?"

"No," she coughed, clearing her throat. "No. I want to be away from here. His name was Robbie, and he said…he said my father didn't die of any illness. That there was an argument, Papa was stabbed, and it was something to do with…" she frowned hard, trying to remember. "Herman… Her many…no…oh, he said something else and it was so noisy and the soldiers—"

"Right. I see," Brand replied in a tone that suggested he didn't see at all. Which was fair, the tale did sound rather farfetched. If she hadn't experienced it in person she probably wouldn't have believed it either.

"No, you didn't. You d-didn't see Robbie get crushed by a c-cart. Before he died, he told me to run, that the guards meant me harm, so that is when I did. I ran and ran, only slowing down when I got near the Grand Duke. Then you pulled me into the alley."

Brand muttered something under his breath but said nothing further, and she realized another man had fallen into step with them. Not nearly as tall as Brand, and nowhere near as broad, but imposing all the same. Actually, not a man, but a lad, dark-haired, dark-eyed and vaguely familiar.

"I've seen you before. At the palace," she said slowly. "You're Lucas de Vere?"

The lad bowed, actually taking her hand and brushing a light kiss over her knuckles as though they were meeting at a banquet. "Indeed, and humbly at your service, beautiful lady! Not impressed by the events of this day, not one bit. To think, such a jewel put in harm's—"

"Lucas," said Brand, rather sharply, as they stopped outside a long stone walkway with heavy iron gates. "This is neither the time nor place. Now hurry and open the gate; the heavens are about to open."

Lucas removed a key from his pocket and attended to a heavy lock, beckoned them both within the high walls and down a gravel path, then secured it again. Beyond a well-manicured lawn stood a large and very beautiful building fashioned of red brick and dark wood timber.

"Always the time or place to compliment a beautiful woman," said Lucas loftily. "Even one looking like she's fought an angry barn cat. You know, Catherine, if Mama were here, she'd pounce with the wire brush and lye soap like she does to my brothers and sisters. I was always too fast to be caught."

Brand scowled.

"If your mother were here, Henry Lucas de Vere, she would drag you by the ear back to Cornwall until you learned to hold your damned tongue. *Mistress Linwood* is in no need of your opinion."

"Mistress Linwood is too long for me to remember. I'm only fourteen, sir."

At the boy's owl-eyed look, she almost smiled. Jane had mentioned exploits of the infamous Lucas de Vere a few times, with a head shake and fond grin. He'd lasted only five weeks in the home of her brother, Norfolk, and now she knew why.

"Speaking of lye soap," she said quickly, as Brand carried her inside the house and set her down on a colorful woven foyer rug, "after that alley I'm in desperate need of a hot bath if you would be so kind as to order one for me, Brand."

He nodded and motioned to two servants, who bowed and dashed away.

Lucas appeared beside her and raised an interested eyebrow. "What happened in the alley, Catherine? I was at the Grand Duke, distracting three men carrying a few too many weapons for a simple luncheon—"

"Cease, boy!" snarled Brand. "I'll speak with you later."

"But—"

"*Go.*"

Lucas grinned widely, lifted her hand and brushed another kiss over her knuckles, then loped away. If he somehow remained un-maimed, no doubt in the future he would shatter hearts all over England and beyond.

Catherine cleared her throat. "He is…"

"There are no adequate words for Lucas," said Brand shortly. "Now, if you'll come with me, I'll show you to a guest chamber. Rest, and later someone will be up with a tray for your supper. I'm afraid you'll have to make do with one of my mother's nightgowns."

Stung by the impersonal words and tone, she followed him up a surprisingly wide wooden staircase to the second floor, along a portrait and tapestry-lined hallway to a spacious, well-appointed chamber overlooking the now rain-lashed Thames.

"Aren't you going to come back?"

His emerald gaze froze her to the floor. "No. You need plenty of rest, Catherine. After tonight…I'm not sure when you'll have it again."

If he were a godly man, he'd have been in the chapel on his knees for the past four hours. As a fully fledged sinner, he'd paced his library, emptied several jugs of wine, and ignored a tray of roasted chicken and freshly baked bread. How could Catherine possibly believe anyone other than the queen had instructed the soldiers? Her innocence and blind faith were both endearing and infuriating. And now, thanks to his brainless intervention, she slept upstairs instead of in a dark dungeon. Yes, they did have a temporary respite—the way the wind and rain were attacking the narrow windowpanes, there'd be no armed invasion of his home tonight—but dawn would bring a brutal reckoning. If not Mary's men then Arundel's creatures. His father's spies seemed to discover news before anyone else, and family meant nothing when there was a monarch's favor to be gained.

Gripping a wine goblet so hard his knuckles whitened, Brand swore softly and took a long swallow. Then another.

He was only halfway to a drunken stupor, and it couldn't come fast enough. Maybe then he'd have a vision or conjure up some miraculous way to get Catherine and himself away from London before they were dragged to the Tower or had a sudden mishap with a street cart.

"Brand?"

With deliberate care, he turned slowly from the roaring fire that offered warmth and light but no comfort from the chills dancing up and down his spine. God's blood. Instead of being safely tucked under a heap of embroidered quilts, Catherine stood in his library doorway wearing a simple linen nightgown created for a figure both less curvaceous and taller than she.

"You should be abed, Catherine."

"You sound different. Have you…have you been drinking?"

The gentle reproof in her voice made him want to down several more jugs of wine. "Most astute of you."

"I had a few sips of wine, but I still couldn't sleep," she said, twisting the folds of the nightgown in her hands until it pulled taut over her breasts, and his cock stirred. "I keep seeing Robbie's face. The man who warned me. And…the cart that accidentally ran him down."

He snorted. "Yes. Accidentally."

"You don't think it was?"

"Don't be a fool," he snapped, angry at her naivety, furious at himself again for the wayward direction of his thoughts and the unwanted reaction of his body. "There is a mystery cloaking your father's death, and a great many people are striving to ensure it stays unsolved. To the point of wishing you ill as well."

"The men with the weapons Lucas mentioned…they

were waiting for me, weren't they?"

"Quite possibly," he said bluntly, perching on the corner of his desk to halt the ridiculous pacing. "To what end, I'm not sure. Perhaps they merely wish to examine you, find out what you know."

Her shuddering gasp was overloud, even against the crackle and spit of the fire and the storm raging outside. "Then I've placed you and Lucas in terrible danger. If they know you helped me today—"

"They know. Every other Londoner is secretly in someone's service. Always assume your enemy is swifter and smarter and progress from there."

"Brand," she said softly, hurrying forward.

Hell. Her unfettered breasts were bobbing under the nightgown with the movement. How easy it would be to undo the narrow ties, to shove the garment from her shoulders and kiss and suck her nipples until she arched her back and begged for more. What color might they be? Palest pink? Dark rose? A dusky brown?

Draining his goblet, he held up an unsteady hand. "Don't. Just go back upstairs, Catherine. Now. Sleep is imperative, we may need to leave before dawn."

She ignored the order, stepping closer and closer until he could smell the lemon scent of her hair, see the wild pulse beating in her throat. Then soft fingers closed around his arm and a jolt of heat tore through him.

"Please don't drink anymore. Please."

"Oh, you're my conscience now? My confessor, perhaps? Forgive me, Saint Catherine, for I am beyond redemption."

"*Brand.*"

"Just leave!"

But she stood her ground, cheeks red yet chin raised defiantly. "Y-you are not my father. And I'm not l-leaving until you explain that kiss in the alley."

"A ruse to fool the guards. Nothing more."

"So you don't wish to kiss me again?"

His cock surged at the thought of that and so much more. No. He couldn't. She was Arthur's only child. His friend's precious daughter. A pure, gentle virgin, the last woman in the world for the likes of him.

"I do not. Now go to bed like a good girl."

Catherine tilted her head and regarded him for a long moment.

"All right," she whispered, and he almost groaned in relief.

Until she went up on her toes and leaned in to brush her lips against his cheek. The first was swift, like greeting a friend. The second time her mouth lingered, opening slightly and releasing a tiny puff of warm air against his jaw.

Brand stilled. "If you play with fire, you will get burned. I'm not a green boy. I'm not a damned courtier to stop at honeyed words, poems, and hot looks while dancing. And I'm certainly no gentleman. I'm a bastard, Catherine. In every sense—my mother was never married to my father. I have no honor to uphold. Arthur was the angel on my shoulder, and he is gone. Stay here and I will spread you across that desk and take you again and again for my own base pleasure because that is what I am. Darkness. Dangerous. If you value your maidenhead, go from here *now*."

She stared at him, her eyes huge sapphire pools. "I know well you are no boy. And our parents' faults are not our own. But no gentleman? You showed me kindness when others walked by. No honor? You rescued me from those who meant to take me prisoner or worse. Our Lord blessed — "

"*God*? God had nothing to do with it. I owed your father," he said angrily, unable to bear the trust and affection in her gaze, the slight flush in her cheeks that spoke of a fledgling desire newly recognized. Damned foolish woman. Why didn't she run?

"Perhaps. But I am in your home. There are many other places. To end the obligation, to be free, you only needed to send me away."

"I will," he bit out, turning his head away from her, at the limit of his control. "Tomorrow. To some high-ranking, sober Catholic courtier, born in wedlock, inclined to marry, and not averse to a learned female. And I won't look back. Ever."

Instead of fleeing, either in temper or sorrow, she ran a tentative finger along his stubbled jaw. "Tis true, I can read and write. But would such a perfect husband be wholly content with that, or might he want more? For in the alley today you taught me how little I know of passion."

His control shattered entirely.

One hand jerked up, clamping around Catherine's wrist and pushing it behind her, forcing her closer and at the same time, arching her back. The other slid along the side of her face until his fingers tangled in the curls behind her ear and his thumb could drag across her lower lip. Back and forth until the flesh darkened and plumped, ready for the nip of his teeth and a soothing lick of his tongue.

He wasn't gentle, couldn't be, too inflamed by the feel and taste of her faintly wine-scented mouth as he crushed her lips under his, spurred on by her ragged gasps. But soon it wasn't enough. Not nearly enough for the ravenous need that coursed through his body and hardened his cock to the point of pain.

Never losing contact with her mouth, Brand shifted both hands to her waist, bunching up her nightgown and setting her on top of the desk. He stood between her bared thighs, a glimpsed thatch of dark hair almost his undoing. But no. Not yet. Her breasts had been the nightly torment of nearly a week now, and he would have his full enjoyment of them.

He stepped back, reveling in her small cry of dismay.

"Unfasten your nightgown," he said so roughly, he scarcely recognized his own voice. Tonight he was truly the blackest of devils, tempting, daring an angel to sin. Surely she would say no. Surely she would now flee.

But Catherine's trembling hands reached up to comply, tugging at the ties, shrugging the garment from her shoulders and revealing the rounded tops of creamy-skinned perfection.

He was doomed....

She was committing a terrible sin. One that would have her publicly whipped and shamed as the worst kind of harlot. Not wed, not in bed, not even in a bedchamber. Instead, she sat perched on a smooth wooden desk, linen nightgown bunched around her spread thighs, elbows pinned to her sides and breasts partially revealed.

Catherine sucked in a shaky breath. And yet the queen's entire army couldn't have moved her from this place. After what Brand had done for her, what he'd risked to save her life, she desperately wanted to offer something in return. And he desired her, even as he battled against it. His kiss just now…she'd thought no kiss in the world could be more seductive, more demanding, more intoxicating than the one in the alley.

No woman could be more wrong.

She felt bewitched, like her overheated, trembling body was no longer her own, and would obey Brand's every instruction without question. Frightening for her first taste of true passion, but at the same time exciting beyond measure.

"Catherine."

Glancing up, she met his gaze and shivered. He'd told her the truth; darkness and danger swirled in the fathomless, molten emerald depths of his eyes.

"Y-yes?"

"Either go, or take your nightgown off. All the way."

Her cheeks ablaze, she shrugged again and the nightgown fell to her waist, her nipples puckering slightly without any protection against the coolness of the evening air.

Brand reached up to cup her breasts, weighing their heavy fullness in his hands. Then his thumbs brushed across the tender tips, and she gasped.

"I…"

"Pale pink now," he murmured, rubbing back and forth over the hardening peaks. "I wonder what hue after?"

"After? After wh…ohh," she said, embarrassed at the choked moan that escaped as his touch grew firmer. He alternated the stroking of her swollen nipples with a delicate thumb and forefinger pinch until they were so engorged and sensitive she could scarcely bear the delicious torment, until she couldn't remain still on the polished desk.

He smiled and lowered his head. Surely he wouldn't…

But he did, and a soft whimper broke from her lips when

his tongue circled one aching nipple then lashed across the turgid peak. Over and over he repeated the action, until finally he took it in his mouth and sucked hard, every tug sending a shard of pure desire straight to her dampening core.

Her cries of delight were overloud in the room, her hands unable to do anything but tangle in his brown hair, anything to hold him to her and ensure he never stopped. Nothing she'd read, nothing she'd seen of hasty corner fumblings could have prepared her for this scorching reality, surely the guiltiest pleasure of all.

"Darkest rose, sweet Carey," he murmured gruffly as his head moved between her breasts, the stubble on his jaw a sensual contrast to the smoothness of his lips and tongue. "So sweet."

Eventually his hand slid a hot path down her side, coming to rest on her uncovered thigh. While his mouth continued its lush teasing of her nipples, his fingers began stroking the soft skin of her inner thigh. Around and around his thumb circled, inching steadily closer to the place burning for ease.

"Please," she begged, intoxicated by the wicked promise in his touch.

Slowly his fingers trailed to her core, and lightly stroked the tight, moisture-soaked curls there. "So wet for me. So hot."

It felt so good she was unable to think, unable to feel shock or mortification at his words, her mind wholly focused on her body's desperate need for something, anything to ease the unbearable ache between her legs. Then his thumb brushed a kernel of flesh so sensitive, she shuddered and moaned at the jolt of fierce pleasure.

"I know, sweetheart. I know what you need, beautiful Carey."

"Brand!" she gasped, joy at the roughly whispered endearments only enhanced when he cupped her. Slowly, so slowly, palm pressing hard against her mound, his fingers surrounded that slick, swollen nub, rubbing and stroking and lightly pinching, pulling her tighter and tighter toward ecstasy, until finally she reached a point she'd never dreamed existed and shattered, her scream of release echoing in the room.

Head awhirl, panting for air, she stared at Brand in wonder.

He watched her, jaw set, perspiration dotting his forehead and temples. Shy at the intentness of his gaze, she glanced down.

And gulped.

Steeling herself against a strong fear of the unknown, all teachings of the church, the knowledge that her life would again be changed irreversibly from this moment, Catherine lifted her chin and attempted a warm smile of invitation.

"D-do you want me to lie down here? Perhaps I could rest my head on your doublet? I know it is painful the f-first time for you must breach my maidenhead, so might you go s-slowly? No, actually, swiftly. If it is swift then it might not hurt so b-badly. I am not some silly girl, I know where your male part must go. I saw a draw—"

A harsh curse interrupted her babble.

"Brand?" she said, lifting one hand to hesitantly cup his cheek.

He jerked away. "Don't."

"I shouldn't touch you? I'm sorry. I'm very new at this."

"You shouldn't even be here. This is foolish, all wrong.

I'm the…damnation!" he snapped, stepping well back from her and running a violent hand through his hair.

Aghast at the words, she blinked. Tears gathered in her eyes and shivers ran through her body as it rapidly cooled. What had she done wrong? "Brand?"

"Leave me, Catherine, please. Go to your chamber."

"But you—"

"Go!" he roared, a sweep of his arm sending a quill and empty inkpot crashing to the floor.

Humiliation scorching her cheeks, she yanked her nightgown back up over her shoulders, awkwardly slid from the desk, and fled the room. Eyes half-blinded by tears, she didn't stop until she could hurl herself onto the wide bed in the guest chamber and sob into a pillow.

How fast one could travel from the glorious heat of passion to the icy chill of rejection.

Indeed, today had truly been the best and the worst.

Chapter Four

He'd nearly taken a devout virgin, his friend's daughter, on a *desk*.

Stumbling into a chair, Brand winced at the throbbing, unrelieved agony of the hugest erection of his life, while at the same time welcoming the pain as punishment for his unspeakable transgression.

It had been a close thing. He'd enjoyed a few women since Therese's death, but none of those encounters came close to the mindless lust he felt for Catherine. The kiss in the alley revealed a startlingly passionate innocent, willing to submit to him entirely. But this was so much more. Her exquisite body, unwrapped like a and generously offered to him without restriction, without the rigid expectation of gifts and favors in return. About the opposite from Therese. Every hurried, unsatisfying coupling with his wife had been a reluctant bargain struck. Fully dressed, in the dark, and a bleak, tense atmosphere of minimal touching, muttered prayers and her palpable disgust.

But Carey…

Brand closed his eyes and groaned, tortured with visions of her lush nakedness. The way she pleaded and writhed in pleasure when he'd stroked and sucked her nipples, the screaming climax when he'd attended to the swollen, pouting nub between her thighs. God. What would it be like with a finger inside her tight heat? Her musky sweetness drenching his tongue? Carey on her hands and knees, breathlessly urging him on as he took her hard from behind, filled her to overflowing with his seed?

If she belonged to him, he would show her every pleasure. Hold her every night, eventually cradle her rounded belly in his hands as their son or daughter grew strong and healthy within her. For Carey would welcome his child, not get rid of it…

His eyes flew open, the thought like plunging into an icy bath.

Marriage? A child?

Clearly he'd reached his limit of mind-turning events for a day. One marriage was quite enough for any man, to even ponder anything different invited naught but disaster. He might have wealth, but he was no prize. Not to mention Carey's dangerous predicament, a shocking plummet from grace with the queen.

Tapping his fingers on the arm of the chair, Brand stared at the dwindling fire in the hearth. That was the strangest thing of all. The Linwoods had been firm favorites at the Tudor court for years. Arthur had even named his daughter for Mary and the queen's beloved late mother Catherine of Aragon. If Arthur's death wasn't natural causes, what could the good doctor possibly have done to anger Mary so greatly that he would be killed for it, and all evidence concealed?

"One man knew," he muttered aloud. "And fell under a cart, God rest him."

An urgent knock at the library door interrupted his musings.

"Come in," he called, and one of his men appeared in saturated clothing. "Damn, man, look at you. Take some wine, get in front of the fire before you freeze to death."

"No time, Sir Brand. I've come from the palace."

A chill shot down his spine and he leapt to his feet.

"What is it?"

"A small army assembling. They are coming for the lady at first light. You must send her away now, sir, then you can—"

"No. Mistress Linwood goes with me," he said sharply, the words tumbling from his mouth and surprising them both. "Tell the stable hand to ready horses for myself and Master Lucas, and get yourself dry and warm. We travel within the hour."

The servant bowed and hurried away.

Running upstairs, he pounded on Lucas's door and pushed it open. "On your feet, boy, we're away from here."

Lucas scrambled out of bed fully dressed, picked up a scuffed pair of boots and hoisted a bulging satchel onto his shoulder. "Ready."

"Good," he said gruffly, impressed at the lad's foresight.

"I just hope you have a better plan to escape the sovereign than my parents did. Although they were actually within Hampton Court. We have a slight head start and the queen isn't fixed on marrying you...wait, are you planning on deposing King Phillip and wedding Mary yourself? Because that isn't a smart plan at all. She is old and not very pretty. Possibly a little crazy too—"

"No," Brand ground out, unable to suppress a shudder. "Never. Not for all the gold and dukedoms in the kingdom would I wed the queen. Now go downstairs and help with the horses. Mistress Linwood and I will follow anon."

Turning, he strode down the hallway to his own chamber, then swiftly picked up a large oiled leather satchel and packed like a soldier—minimum comfort and maximum practicality. Two changes of hose, undershirt and doublet, and on top he rested several sheathed daggers of various sizes and a large bag of coins. Collecting his most comfortable pair of boots, he took a deep breath and made his way to Catherine's chamber.

Surprisingly, she sat on the edge of the bed, holding her clothing in her arms.

"Catherine," he said, far more curtly than he intended. "Guards are coming from the palace. We must go at once."

"I know," she replied, not meeting his gaze. "I mean, I guessed when I heard you running up the stairs. Might I borrow some clothing? My gown is fit only for burning and my shoes are still in that alley."

He strode past her into a small adjoining room and gathered stockings, petticoat, chemise and corset, a simple dark blue woolen gown, heavy black hooded cloak and a pair of wooden shoes, then returned to the chamber. All the items had belonged to his mother so were several years out of style, but they would be comfortable enough for the journey.

"Here," he said. "I'll help you with your laces."

Catherine fumbled with the garments, holding them against herself as she attempted to remove her nightgown with one hand. "I'm fine, thank you."

"We have not the time for this," he said impatiently. "And there is not one inch of your body I have not seen already."

She finally looked at him then, her expression a war of embarrassment, sorrow, and anger. "You need not remind me of that folly. Please leave."

"Catherine," he said, gentling his tone as much as he was able, "I won't look. But for the love of God, now is not the occasion to fight me."

"Well," she snapped. "Do it then!"

Gritting his teeth, he turned around and stared blankly at the wall, tapping his fingers on his thigh as he listened to the rustle and rasp of clothing being discarded and put on. Actually, she was dressing with admirable speed and efficiency. Therese had always taken hours to get ready, with the help of at least two chambermaids.

"All right?"

"Yes, Sir Brandon."

He turned back. Catherine wore the stockings, chemise and petticoat, and had the corset held up to her front with the laces falling behind her. Before she had time to change her mind he stepped forward and carefully threaded the laces in a crisscross pattern, pulling them tight as he went. Damned annoying things, corsets. Significantly easier to unfasten than fasten. Finally he lifted the gown over her head, knotting the ties at the sides, back, and sleeves.

She stepped into the shoes, fastened a small drawstring bag to the sash at her waist and folded the cloak over her arm. "Where will we go? To your country home? By the by, I must warn you I'm a poor rider."

He stuffed her nightgown into his satchel to gain a

moment to think.

"You'll share with me," he said eventually, his mind racing. There really was only one place they could go. "And no, we won't go to my mother. They will look for us there first. To have any chance of solving this mystery, we must travel to where it began. The town where your father died."

The storm had created havoc in London, the cobbled streets awash with mud, bits of wood and stone, and half-starved animals attacking sacks of grain and ruined market produce. Fortunately for their group of six—her and Brand, Lucas, and three servants with flaming torches to light their way—the sharp-eyed residents in need of coins and ale were sheltering in their homes with doors and shutters securely locked.

It was a painstaking process as the horses stepped around treacherous debris and splashed through deep and murky puddles. Her nerves were permanently on edge as she sat rigidly in the saddle, constantly watching for movement, ears straining in the freezing darkness for any sound not of their making.

"Catherine. If you don't relax, you won't be able to walk later."

She shivered at Brand's whisper in her ear. It was beyond tempting to do so, to lean back against the huge, solid warmth and protection of his chest, tuck her head into his neck again, and be soothed by the rocking motion of the fine thoroughbred's rhythmic gait.

Under no circumstances would she do that. Brand had made it perfectly clear what he thought of her, his utter rejection of her wanton behavior couldn't have been more explicit. She wouldn't give him a single further reason to dislike her, to goad him into abandoning her to the queen's men. "I'm fine, thank you," she muttered, pulling her cloak tighter around her body.

He sighed but said nothing further, and they rode in silence for hours, from the time the first rays of dawn streaked the dark sky, to the point where the winter sun was a pale orb, high above them. On another occasion she might have asked to stop and admire the fresh beauty of the Surrey woods and meadows or the pretty thatched-roof cottages dotting the tranquil landscape. But they were moving at a reasonably brisk trot now. Every mile between them and London offered safety and a much-needed buffer to find answers before anyone else in Guildford knowing the truth about her father's death was silenced forever.

Abruptly, Brand called a halt and guided their mount into a small clearing.

"We'll stop here for a bite to eat. There is bread, cheese, and wine in my saddlebags."

Lucas practically vaulted off his horse toward the food source, and she smiled.

"Save some for me, Lucas," Catherine said, more amused as he rummaged frantically through the bags like a man unfed for weeks. "My stomach has been grumbling this past hour."

"That was your stomach?" said Brand, "I thought surely the thunderclaps of a storm to flatten the entire county—"

He coughed, and she quickly removed her wayward elbow from his flat, hard belly, her cheeks hot. The action had been instinctive, as if he teased her often and she responded in kind.

"I'm sorry," she mumbled, horrified.

Brand dismounted from their horse, digging into another saddlebag for a handful of oats and rubbing the magnificent ebony animal's neck while it ate directly from his palm.

"No you aren't."

"A truth," she snapped, then clamped a hand over her mouth. What on earth was wrong with her? Fortunately the servants were in a circle several feet away, eating their own rations and talking amongst themselves, and didn't witness her lapse.

His gaze met hers, but shockingly, there was no anger there. Just…laughter?

"I shall keep in mind your preferred method of retribution, considering our close proximity for the rest of the journey. Now let's get you fed while there are still crumbs remaining."

Lucas snorted. "Not my fault if you pigeons wish to bill and coo rather than eat. This cheese is tasty."

"That cheese is to feed the three of us, piglet," said Brand, coming around to help her down from the horse. She winced as she touched the ground, her legs cold and cramped from the icy wind that had swirled up and under her petticoat and gown. Stockings were lovely, but she would give all she owned for a pair of thick hose like the men wore.

Gratefully accepting a serving of crusty bread and hard, crumbling cheese, she ate quickly then gulped down several mouthfuls of wine from a flagon. It was a rich burgundy, potent enough to make her eyes water, but the resulting warmth in her belly was sheer bliss.

A quarter hour later they were on their way again, and she craned her head, looking for any clues of an impending town.

"Are we very far from Guildford, do you think?"

"If we can keep a good pace, and barring any injuries to the horses, I think we should reach there by late tomorrow afternoon."

"As long as that?" she said, blinking in surprise and dismay. "I thought the town was little more than a day's hard ride from London."

"Perhaps in summertime, when the road is firm and dry. When it's muddy and rutted like this, it is far too dangerous to gallop, a horse could break a leg or slip and throw its rider. We'll find a place to make camp for the night, my men have sheets of canvas and wooden pegs to fashion into several tents. And wool blankets for warmth. It will be a bit damp and uncomfortable, but adequate."

"When we reach Guildford, can we look straight away for Robbie's family?"

"Yes," he said, skillfully guiding their mount around a section of muddy, cart-gouged road. "Hopefully we'll have time to find an adequate inn and walk the town to make some enquiries before darkness sets in. Best to start in the area where your father treated his noble patients. It is difficult this time of year, we really are limited in hours of daylight, and in our current situation it's not safe to be wandering a place we don't know."

Catherine couldn't control a shudder. "Brand...I..."

"I know this is a terrifying predicament to be in. But I won't let anyone hurt you," he said softly, his lips so close to her ear they occasionally brushed it. She briefly closed her eyes at the blessed promise, even as a wave of mortifying desire gripped her. It seemed her body refused to listen to reason, refused to remember his utter rejection in the library no matter how vividly her mind recalled it.

"I just don't want anything bad to happen to you because of me. You've already done so much to help me, when you owe me nothing."

For a moment, his arms tightened around her waist, as if she'd said something entirely objectionable.

"Arthur…you're Arthur's daughter," he said finally, his voice oddly flat. "For that reason alone, I owe you everything. Perhaps you don't know all he did for me, but saving my mother's life was just the beginning. I was on a dark path after my wife died, so in many ways he saved my life, too."

Catherine froze as the word repeated over and over in her head, almost to the beat of the horse's hooves.

Wife. Wife. Wife.

"Y-you were married?" she choked out.

There was a long pause, so long she dreaded his answer more.

"Yes, to Lady Therese Fairfax, for a short while," he said curtly. "We'd only been wed six months when she…when she died unexpectedly. That's nearly five years ago now."

Nausea roiled in her belly. She'd never met Therese. The blond beauty had been several years older and her superior in all ways: elegant, charming, the pride of an ancient and wealthy Catholic family. But she remembered the lady's passing, mourned by an entire court it seemed.

No wonder in all that time Brand had never remarried.

No wonder he'd sent her away from his library.

He was still desperately in love with his dead wife.

The light was fading fast now, so fast even the pretty woodlands were turning a dull gray, but they'd found a decent place to stop for the night. About a quarter mile from the road, the site boasted a small, relatively flat clearing cunningly hidden behind a dense group of trees and a narrow, knee-deep stream nearby for water.

Under the guise of rubbing down the horses, Brand let his forehead rest briefly on a warm flank.

God's blood he was tired. Not to mention in desperate need of a few barrels of wine, and to lose himself completely in the sweet, hot depths of an experienced woman. Anything to take his mind off Catherine Linwood. It was definitely a good thing he'd told her about Therese. Now she had pieced the story together, she would keep her distance, safe in her disgust, in her horror at the truth of what he was.

"Sir Brand! Supper is ready," called one of his men, and he waved a hand to show he was on his way.

Securing each of the horses to a low, long branch, he ambled back toward the fire where the rest of the party sat devouring chunks of bread coated in cheese that Catherine had prepared. She hadn't stopped. Not for a moment. Over and over he'd been reminded how useful women outside the nobility were, as she'd gathered wood for a fire, set a pot to boil water, even expertly bandaged Lucas's palm when he scraped it on a stray tent peg.

"That food smells good," he said, dropping down onto a fallen log.

Catherine immediately handed him two large chunks of

the bread. "I hope so. I can make more, although we might want to save some for breakfast."

"Have you eaten?"

"I will in a minute. I just need to—"

"Sit down, Catherine."

Reluctantly, she perched on the log beside him and nibbled at her own supper.

"Are you happy with the tents, Sir Brand?" said Lucas, crouching to stoke the fire.

Glancing over, he admired the three makeshift shelters. They'd draped sheets of dark green canvas over thick branches, securing the bottom edge to the ground with sturdy wooden pegs through small brass circles, and smaller sheets had been unrolled inside the structures to act as a floor. There was definitely something to be said for employing ex-soldiers.

"Excellent work."

"What are we going to do tonight?" said Catherine. "Will someone keep watch?"

All the men paused and looked at him expectantly.

"We'll take shifts," said Brand decisively. "I'll take the first, then you lot decide amongst yourselves who will stand guard until morning. You are free to rest after supper, I want us to be packed up and back on the road to Guildford at daybreak."

Over the next few hours they played cards, but eventually his men and Lucas abandoned the game for bed. Soon, he and Catherine sat alone on a fallen log, hands stretched toward the fire for warmth, with a heavy woolen blanket covering their legs and cloaks securely fastened around their shoulders. Even so, the seeping chill numbed his toes and ears, and tiny white clouds danced in front of him when he breathed.

Catherine shivered and wrapped her arms around her stomach.

"Saints be praised this is only for one night."

He nodded. "Arthur would not approve of our outdoor sojourn. Actually, I don't think the horses approve either. Far too used to their warm stables and unending supply of oats and hay."

"You are very good with them. Did your father teach you?"

Before he thought to temper his reaction, he'd recoiled, his fists clenching. "No."

"I'm so sorry, that was awful of me. You don't have to say anything," she said, and he forced himself to meet her embarrassed gaze. Clearly she'd just remembered what he'd told her in his library about his illegitimacy.

Perhaps it was the intimacy of the campsite so far away from London, perhaps just his utter weariness, but beyond all reason, he wanted to tell her about his upbringing.

"It's a long story," he said hesitantly.

"Well, we do have a few hours to occupy until the next watch takes over. If you want to share, I mean."

Brand took a deep breath.

"I only met my father five years ago," he began. "He is a wealthy nobleman who sowed his wild oats as a page in King Henry's court and turned his back on a rather naive young lady when she told him of her pregnancy. His relatives were most displeased and made terrible trouble for my mother, but fortunately her own family forgave the sin and took her back, babe and all. My grandfather oversaw my studies, and my uncle, a soldier, taught me how to ride, fish, and handle a sword."

"How wonderful you had them. I bet you were a rough-and-tumble boy."

"Indeed I was. There were a few village lads who joined in on the odd adventure, but most weren't permitted to speak to me or my mother because of the scandal of my birth. She was too well-known for it to be hidden, and gossip travels remarkably well."

Catherine flinched. "Do you still see your grandfather and uncle often?"

An old arrow of pain delved deep, and he took a moment to watch the bright yellow flames and orange sparks of the campfire for composure.

"Unfortunately, they both passed long ago. That is why when my mother fell ill, I was determined she have the best doctor in England, Arthur Linwood. I do not care for my true father, but his connections enabled me to secure Arthur's expertise, and that is a service I shall not forget."

Catherine made a muffled sound, and he jerked his head around. Her eyes remained dry, but she was biting her plump lower lip hard.

"He was the best. Wasn't he? Not a b-butcher."

Unthinkingly, he reached over and took her hand in his. "Those guards were fools, spreading practiced lies. Never believe anything other than your father had a remarkable gift for healing."

"Papa helped so many people. He didn't care whether they were nobleman, farmer, or fishwife. But sometimes I had selfish thoughts. So selfish I had to attend confession twice as often."

His lips twitched at the grave tone. "Really?"

"I wished…I wished he weren't quite so good, because he was always being called away to tend the sick. When he was home, we would go for walks around London and eat pasties from stalls. In our rooms he would read aloud and teach me things so I could assist in examinations. Sometimes I was so lonely without him I thought it might break me. Courtiers are too…changeable…to be true friends."

Hell. Brand turned back to the campfire. He didn't want open honesty, no knowledge they might have much in common despite their very different lives. Even sitting here speaking of the past and cradling her hand was madness.

The brutal lust that coursed through his body whenever he thought about the alley kiss or interlude in his library was bad enough. But to succumb to deeper feelings, to allow lust to become something more would be the worst mistake of his mistake-riddled life. He had to concentrate on solving the mystery of Arthur's death and keep Catherine safe until she found the husband she deserved. He must definitely not think of her sitting near a fire in a far different location, smiling and talking as she nursed a brown-haired babe at her breast…

"Brand!"

He blinked. "What is the matter?"

"You're crushing my hand."

"Sorry," he said quickly, dropping it and folding his arms.

"I won't talk about myself anymore, I promise. Tell me… tell me about your mother instead. Is she well?"

Brand sighed in relief at the easier topic.

"Very much so. But she chooses to remain in the country, on our lands in West Berkshire. I would stay there too. London…court life…is not for me."

"I understand. When I was a child, Papa was the personal physician to Lord Clinton and his family."

"Bessie Blount's husband?"

"Don't say it like that, she was wonderfully kind to my mother and me. I often played with the Clinton girls, and attended their lessons when Papa went away with the baron. They traveled everywhere, France, Scotland, and told us jaw-dropping tales on their return. I didn't want to leave when we were summoned to court, but Papa was renowned for his doctoring by then."

"Do you keep in touch with Baron Clinton?"

"Not really. He's so busy, and up to his third wife now!"

"Foolish man," he said laughing, only to halt when a discreet cough sounded.

Glancing up in surprise, he saw two servants ready to take up watch duties. Had he and Catherine really been talking for so long?

Slowly rising, grimacing as his numb feet refused to walk without stumbling, he guided Catherine into her tent.

"Take this," he said, unfolding a blanket as she settled onto the rock-hard ground. "Try and get some rest."

"Where will you be?"

Brand hesitated, his reply stalling at her pale cheeks, the tremor in her voice.

"Here. I'll be here," he said instead, wanting to give himself a hard shake even as he spread out a second blanket and lay down on the opposite side of the tent. Reason had fled the day he met Catherine Linwood, so what was one more foolish act?

She smiled gratefully and closed her eyes, but his

remained wide open.

A mere foot away lay the most luscious temptation he had ever known. And somewhere out beyond the trees, a small army might even now be closing in with deadly intent.

A more accurate definition of heaven and hell, he couldn't imagine.

Chapter Five

"Catherine. Wake up."

Keeping her eyes firmly shut, she shook her head and burrowed further into her deliciously warm bed. The pillowcase was coarser than she remembered, but that hardly mattered, not when she felt so wonderfully content. Safe.

Sighing happily, Catherine stretched and flexed against the firm mattress. It rubbed nicely against her breasts and that forbidden place between her legs, too nice really, and she couldn't help doing it again.

"For the love of God, woman. *Wake up.*"

She frowned. Her bed was talking. And in pain?

One eyelid inched open. It took a moment to adjust to the gloomy darkness barely tempered by a pale beam of light, but with awareness came pure embarrassment.

Sweet heaven. She was in a tent and actually lying on top of Brand, her breasts pressed hard against his massive chest and her legs partially spread by one muscular thigh. The coarse pillowcase was his cloak.

"I'm sorry!" Catherine gasped, face flaming and hands flailing as she attempted to untangle her gown and cloak and climb off him.

Hands gripped her waist like a vice.

"Stop. *Wriggling.*"

Confused by Brand's rough tone, his short, panting breaths, she lifted slightly and stared down at him. And felt the bulge nudging her left hip.

Oh.

Gulping a harsh breath of her own, she didn't say a word as he grimaced and shifted, his body rigid with tension beneath her. Intrigued, she turned her head downward and watched in rapt fascination as the bulge hardened and lengthened.

Wickedly unbidden, her left hand slid down and stroked him, once then twice.

Brand groaned, his back arching to force his male part harder against her palm, but just as quickly, fingers clamped around her wrist and pulled her away.

"Don't! What are you doing?" she said. "Please, let me, ahh!—"

The indignant yelp tore from her throat as in one swift, mind-spinning movement, he half-lifted and set her well away from him.

"No."

"But why?" she said boldly. "You...you wanted me to touch you, I know you did."

"And you know so little of men. That often happens in the morning...and any woman will do."

In another place, in another tone, the comment would have been a dagger to the heart. But Brand was so tense, his hands uncharacteristically clumsy as he attempted to yank one boot onto the wrong foot, and without unfastening the buckle.

"Oh really?" she said slowly, deliberately lifting the hem of her gown to her knees to smooth her stockings and put on her own shoes. "Any woman?"

His eyes closed briefly. "Damnation, Carey. I can't. I bloody can't. Besides, when this is all over, when you're back in London safe, well, and in favor again, you'll feel differently and be very glad I said no."

Carey.

Heart lifting, Catherine shuffled onto her knees, leaned toward him, and let her fingertips caress his chest. "You think I could just forget everything that has happened? Well, I will not. That my affection is so fickle? No, it is not. That there might be a day when I do not dream of the way you kissed me, your touch on my breasts or between my legs when you showed me such pleasure? You ask too much."

For the longest moment he stared at her, his gaze hot and hungry. One hand tucked a stray curl behind her ear, the light, brief caress making her whimper.

Kiss me, Brand. Please, please, kiss me.

He cleared his throat. "It's getting light. We have to get back on the road to Guildford. I'll go and fetch some washing water."

And with that, he scrambled out of the tent and marched away.

Tears stung her eyes, but she refused to let them fall. Instead, she concentrated fiercely on re-plaiting her hair, brushing her clothing as best she could and once outside, toasting the last of the bread and cheese for the men's breakfast. An hour later they were packed up and on their way, but Brand hardly spoke a word for the rest of the day's journey, even holding himself rigidly on their horse so he barely touched her.

When they finally entered the town of Guildford, she—and her aching backside—nearly cheered in relief. A town square had never looked so good, the thought of escaping the bleak and chilly afternoon for an inn with soft beds, roaring fire, mulled wine, and food other than bread or cheese, making her squirm.

"Sir Brand," said Lucas, pulling up beside them, his young mount stepping and dropping its head in sheer fatigue. "What do you propose, an inn first or scatter to see what we can discover about Doctor Linwood? Is there a certain area? A family we must look for?"

Brand shifted in the saddle behind her.

"We haven't much time before nightfall, so I think we tie up the horses then scatter. We are looking for the family of Robbie Blacksmith. He was the last person to see Arthur alive."

"Why don't we just ask Robbie?"

Catherine shuddered and crossed herself, as once again the memory of the young man's gruesome death clawed her mind and heart. "Because Robbie is dead, Lucas. He was pushed in front of a cart by the soldiers for warning me of danger."

The lad's dark eyes widened. "Oh. *Oh*. Well. I must say, Catherine, it would surely help if you told us what your father did—"

"Lucas!" Brand hissed.

"It would help," said Lucas, his expression stormy. "Because this doesn't seem like a small thing such as…I don't know… kissing the queen's maids or besting her favorite in a tournament. She is so angry. And two people are dead already."

Sick despair slumped her shoulders.

"That is the problem," she said hoarsely. "I don't know what he did. Or said."

"He might not have done or said anything," snapped Brand as he slid off the horse. "We all know court rumors are often wrong, yet swiftly spread by those with a grudge or someone wanting to usurp a position. Tis a viper's nest at the best of times. But we won't get to the truth until we find Robbie's relatives. Let's pair off and search. We'll stable the horses at that inn over there, and meet again at dusk."

Brand quickly secured lodgings and supper from the smilingly deferential innkeeper who came outside to greet them. Then the other four men left to begin the search for Robbie's family.

Catherine wrapped her arms around herself, discreetly flexing muscles cramped and sore from sitting in a saddle for the best part of two days and sleeping on the hard ground. Now they were here in Guildford, she wished she were anywhere else.

Her eyes had been opened to a different world, one of the glorious pleasures that might be found between a man and woman, certainly, but now she also knew much of dark and ugly matters. Of violent deaths, merciless orders, and cruel lies. Surely Mary didn't know of these evil deeds. How could she?

And yet, a devil of doubt whispered, *how could she not?*

"Catherine? Are you well? You've gone very pale."

"I'm afraid," she admitted reluctantly, almost unable to meet Brand's steady gaze. "Being here, it makes everything so real. That Papa is never coming back, and my desire to find the truth might put even more lives in danger. What if we discover something truly a-awful, either about my father or—"

"The queen," he finished bluntly. "I strongly suspect the latter."

"Oh, of course you do. But you've never even met her, Brand! How do you think this is for me, knowing someone I loved and served my whole life could have…"

Unable to even say the wicked, sinful words, she buried her face in her hands.

Brand cursed, and she wept harder at the thought of him angry with her, until he hauled her into his arms and stroked her hair.

"Don't cry, Carey," he said gruffly, his lips just brushing her cheek. "I would know the truth as much as you. We'll find it, I know we will. And whatever it is, you won't be alone."

Held tightly against his warm, hard chest, she almost believed him.

How many Blacksmiths could there be in one bloody town?

It was increasingly difficult to keep a smile on his face as they were politely fare-thee-welled from yet another unrelated family. He and Catherine had been trudging up and down the narrow, muddy streets of Guildford for hours now, even along the river Wey and as far up as the sternly imposing Guildford Castle. Several times it seemed like they had gained a promising snippet of information, only for it to lead nowhere.

"It's no use," said Catherine miserably, her steps dragging heavily in the borrowed wooden shoes. "We'll never find Robbie's family. And it's getting dark."

Brand gritted his teeth, hating to admit defeat, but she was right. The night offered an enemy both cover and an easy escape; while they weren't being followed at present, people were beginning to watch them and he didn't want to risk Catherine's safety in a surprise attack. "We *will* find them. Perhaps not tonight, but in the morning. Besides, the others might have news and even now the right family could be waiting for us."

"How…how long do you think we have?"

"I don't know. We traveled discreetly and with a destination in mind. Guildford may not be the soldiers' first choice, but I still wouldn't dare expect any more than a few days."

"And then I'll be arrested. Do you think the Tower, Brand? Or—"

"No," he growled, coming to a halt on the footpath, taking her cool hands in his and chafing them. "I won't let them take you. Understand?"

Catherine stared up at him, her ashen cheeks only emphasizing the deep blue of her eyes, the soft pink of her lips. Unable to resist, he lifted his other hand and traced her trembling lower lip with his thumb.

"I understand," she replied softly, and in one swift movement she tilted her head so he cupped her cheek. Then she turned, her gaze never leaving his, and kissed his open palm.

Sensation sparked through him, and he sucked in a harsh breath. How much temptation could one sinner be expected to take?

Not even an icy stream plunge had been enough to quell his cock after Catherine used him as her feather bed, and the saddle tortured him the rest of the journey. Now when she looked at him with those huge, thickly-lashed eyes and kissed him, it took every ounce of control he had not to drag her into another alley and take her until he collapsed.

"Let's go back to the inn," he said, lust roughening his tone to a near-growl. "I'm sure you would welcome some food and wine."

Fortunately they weren't far away from the inn, and Lucas and his men were already there. They dined in a private room for supper, generous in size and well scrubbed with freshly scented herbal water. The meal of thick beef and vegetable stew, chunks of brown bread and a light, fruity wine was also surprisingly excellent, but while he, Lucas, and the servants cleaned their plates, Catherine barely managed a few mouthfuls.

Brand leaned closer to her. "Is the food not to your liking? Do you want me to order something else?"

She gave him a wan smile. "The food is fine. I'm not especially hungry."

"Not hungry?" said Lucas, as though Catherine spoke in a foreign tongue. "Can't believe it. Actually another thing I can't believe, the sheer number of Blacksmiths in Guildford. Clearly too many long, cold nights in this town with naught to do but f— Ow! Who kicked me?"

"Can't imagine," Brand said, with a warning glare.

"Well," said the lad, looking vastly offended, "I shall venture into the taproom and see if I can find out anything further under the guise of relieving ungodly card players of their ill-gotten gains. Anyone without unruly donkey limbs care to join me?"

His men looked to him for permission, and he sent them away with a handful of groats and a stern warning against drunkenness or brawling. The last thing they needed was the townspeople hauling them away to the local noble magistrate.

Catherine yawned delicately. "Oh, dear. Excuse me."

"It's been a very long day. Shall I escort you to your chamber?"

"If you wouldn't mind."

He nodded and guided her from the room, up two sets of narrow wooden stairs and along a candle-lit hallway to the last door on the left. The chamber was small but clean, with a roaring fire, quilted bed, two wooden tables with lit candles atop, several iron hooks for clothing, and a screened-off corner probably containing a chamber pot and washing water. His satchel sat on the bed, an undershirt and Catherine's nightgown spread out next to it.

"I'll take that," he said quickly, stepping forward. "The innkeeper's wife must have assumed we were married."

"Brand…"

He turned his head, frowning at her unsteady tone, the way her hands were twisting her gown. "What's wrong? You'll be perfectly safe, I promise. Lock the door, and I'll sleep outside on a pallet—"

"Please…" she whispered. "Don't leave me alone tonight."

His doublet suddenly too tight around his neck, Brand

looked anywhere but at her. Another night with her so close? He couldn't.

"Catherine—"

"I beg you."

"Damnation, I…very well. I'll sit here, just until you fall asleep."

"Thank you," she said, her cheeks pink. "Could you… also unlace me?"

Swiftly, impersonally, not daring to linger, he withdrew his small boot dagger and cut the end of the ties binding her sleeves and sides then lifted the blue woolen gown over her head. The garment was thick with dust, the hem caked in mud, but she'd not complained once. Next he unfastened her corset, until it fell forward into her hands and she put it to one side.

Snatching up the nightgown, Catherine disappeared behind the screen and soon he heard the small splashes of a hasty sponge bath.

After removing his boots and cloak, Brand stretched out on top of the bed and closed his eyes as a powerful wave of weariness surged through him.

"Does your head ache?" said Catherine, as she slid under the quilts beside him.

"No, I'm fine. Rest now, you've earned it."

"All right. Good night, Brand."

"Good night."

How long he dozed, he wasn't sure. But when he opened his eyes again, only one candle remained burning and the fire had halved in size. Yet he wasn't cold. Mainly because, like the previous night in the tent, Catherine lay curled against him, one arm flung over his chest and her lush breasts pressed closely to his side.

His cock hardened, throbbing painfully. He needed to get out of here or cool his raging blood at least. Carefully extracting himself from her embrace, Brand padded across the room to the screened corner, removed his doublet, undershirt and hose, and washed himself with the pleasantly tepid water. Unfortunately the slightly rough sponge around his cock did not have the desired effect, the light friction only making him harder.

He groaned softly, reaching down and encircling his erection. The need to come was now an urgent, desperate thing, then perhaps he could sleep peacefully for the first time since he'd met Catherine Linwood. No other woman had affected him as much, her laughter, her tears, her frankness, the perfection of her body.

Closing his eyes, he squeezed and rubbed as he remembered her rose-tipped breasts, the soft, dark hair between her thighs, the slick, swollen nub he'd played with until she screamed her pleasure…

"Brand?"

He jerked at the too-close soft voice, one hand bracing on the wall as he spun away.

"Damnation," he half snarled, half gasped, his hugely swollen cock nearly resting on his stomach. "What is the matter, Catherine?"

"Are you all right? I heard sounds, and you weren't on the bed."

"Fine. Just…bathing. I'll be there soon."

There was a long, long pause, and he inhaled unsteadily. His cock was so painfully engorged that veins were visible even in this low light, and drops of moisture were trickling from the head to ease the path of his hand. Just a few more minutes would end the pulsing, unbearable ache.

Go. Please, for the love of God, go.

Yet instead of retreating footsteps, the next sound he heard was water dripping from a lifted sponge. Then it brushed softly against his back.

Brand tensed, gritting his teeth.

"What are you doing?"

"I thought that might be obvious. Washing your back," she replied, dragging the wet sponge up the length of his spine, across his shoulders, then down, down until it caressed the top of his backside.

More warm seed spilled from his cock at the innocent torture. "Good. I'm fine," he choked out eventually. "Thank you. Now go back to bed."

Again, the longest of pauses.

"No," she whispered, raising a cool hand to give him a gentle push. "Turn around."

Would he do it?

Every part of her silently begged him to. Not even the fading light of the unstoked fire or single remaining candle disguised the beauty of his male body. She'd seen backs before, even partially uncovered limbs while assisting her father, but no masculine form compared to Brand's huge, powerful shoulders, tight, flat buttocks, and strong, muscled legs.

She squirmed at the dampness between her thighs, her nightgown chafing her peaking nipples like it was fashioned of sackcloth. Again, she pushed his shoulder, knowing she teased a lion and unable to stop herself.

Brand swore, finally, slowly turning to face her.

Oh.

Riveted, she stared at his brawny chest, lightly dusted with dark hair that nearly covered two flat, pale brown male nipples. No extra fat marred the sculpted lines of his abdomen, but that was naught in comparison to the magnificence of the long, thick male part resting against his palm. It stood nearly upright from a nest of black hair, pale-colored moisture coating the hugely swollen head as well as his fingers.

One wayward finger reached out and halted.

"May I..." she swallowed, finally meeting his molten emerald gaze. "May I touch it?"

One tiny jerk of his head gave her permission. Emboldened, she stepped closer and stroked him from base to tip, marveling at the hardness, the smoothness of the skin, the silky texture of his seed.

He groaned. "Catherine..."

"Am I hurting you?"

"No. Just torturing me."

"What should I do?"

"To be fair and equal, be as naked as I am."

A grim smile twitched her lips. Tonight she didn't feel like a virginal physician's daughter on the run from the queen's soldiers, but a woman needing the man who'd dominated her thoughts, her heart, since the day they met.

Untying the front ribbon of her nightgown, she let the garment fall to the floor. His indrawn breath and slow, greedy appraisal of her body a reward for the daring act.

"And now, Brand?"

"Take my cock in your hands and stroke it. Like this," he said, wrapping her hands tightly around the length of him and moving them back and forth.

Eagerly she complied, exulting in his choked sighs and incoherent words as he thrust against her fingers. Wanting to get closer, she dropped to her knees and leaned in, brushing the lightest of kisses across the tip.

He froze and she lifted her head, uncertain. "I'm sorry, I—"

"Don't apologize," he said, so raggedly she felt another rush of moist heat between her legs. "It feels very, very good when a man has his cock kissed. Or licked. Or sucked. If you wish to, do what you will."

"I wish to," she replied, darting her tongue out to taste the musky wetness there.

"God, yes. Like that, Carey. So good."

His gruff praise warmed her to the soul, and lifting her gaze to his, she deliberately held it while taking the wide head of his erection into her mouth. Brand's harsh breaths echoed through the room as she sucked gently, then more firmly, taking him a little deeper and hollowing her cheeks while her fingers teased the underside of his shaft.

"Sweetheart. Carey. Yes, darling. Damn, I'm going to…"

Abruptly a guttural roar tore from the very depths of him, and he jerked his erection from her lips, long streams of warm liquid splashing her breasts and belly, his other hand gripping her shoulder while his body spasmed.

For the longest moment Brand stood like that, his eyes closed and head tilted back, as though a thousand miles away. Then he met her gaze, and the fire there seared her to the core.

Catherine shivered. "Are you going to—"

"Wash you? Yes. Kiss and lick and suck every inch of your beautiful body? Yes. But it won't be swift, Carey. I won't be merciful. Perhaps when dawn comes, when your sweet cream drenches my fingers, and you beg me for release, I may grant it to you. We shall see."

Unable to speak, enthralled by the dark promise of the words, she took his offered hand and got to her feet. Slowly, far too slowly, he washed his seed from her skin. The herbed water wasn't cold, but she shuddered at the contrast on her too-hot flesh, the way the slightly rough sponge grazed her hardened nipples, her belly, the curls between her legs. Soon he discarded the sponge, instead using two fingers to tease her wet flesh.

She gripped his shoulder and sighed, back arching in shock when the fingers slid gently inside her. Quickly he bent his head, taking one nipple into his mouth to suck while starting a rhythm of advance and retreat between her legs certain to steal her wits.

"Please," she begged, as the delicious tingling feeling started low in her belly. "Harder."

"You're so slick here, Carey. So hot," he rasped. Then he stopped.

"*Brand!*"

He didn't reply, just scooped her into his arms and placed her in the center of the bed with her feet dangling over the end. Before she had time to think, he knelt between her spread thighs and bent down to claim her mouth, overwhelming her with his hunger.

"Brand," she gasped, tearing away. "I don't know how."

"Your body does. Listen to it," he replied, but this time his kiss was gentler, coaxing, imploring her to open to him.

Enraptured, she didn't even feel his hand move until two fingers surrounded one tender nipple and lightly pinched. She writhed, moaning as he did it again and again, alternating with a teasing lick. "No," she sobbed, mindless with need. "Touch me properly."

"Where?"

"There," she said, a flailing hand gesturing between her legs.

Brand moved down the bed, and breathlessly she waited for the relief of his fingers stroking, delving inside her. Instead, his lips brushed her inner thigh and trailed upward.

Her hands grasped the sheets tightly.

Surely he wouldn't.

Oh please, let him.

At the first lash of his tongue across her heated core, she attempted to close her legs, the rush of acute pleasure too much to bear. But he was relentless, one shoulder wedging her thighs wide as he lapped and sucked the swollen nub beneath her nether curls, and plunged his tongue deep inside her soaked, aching channel.

She cried out.

"Should I stop?" he teased.

"Nooooo," she wailed, lifting and circling her hips, wanting to claw his back bloody for tormenting her when she craved him so desperately. "Hurry. More. Please."

Brand stilled and lifted his head.

"Do you know what you're asking?" he said, almost angrily. "Do you, Carey? Because once my cock is buried inside you, there is no going back. You will belong to me, body and soul, for always."

Catherine cupped his cheek. "And you'll belong to me. Won't you?"

"God help you," he bit out. "Yes. When we're back in London, I will find a vicar — "

"A *priest*."

"Someone to marry us."

She laughed, as momentarily all the darkness, her sadness and fear, were banished by pure joy. "Then make me yours, Brand. For always."

"In my library you said fast. What about now?"

"The same," she said softly, closing her eyes and grasping the quilt to ready herself.

"No, Carey. Open your eyes."

Brand braced himself on his knees and elbow. One hand laced fingers with hers, the other took his erection and fitted it to her entrance. Seconds later he thrust hard and she muffled a shriek at the tearing pain.

"I'm sorry, sweetheart, I'm sorry," he murmured over and over, utterly still inside her, his taut shoulders and sheened temples revealing the control he exercised.

"It is better now," she whispered and, although she felt overwhelmingly stretched and full, it was.

He began to move, inching inside her then withdrawing, reaching down to fit her legs around his hips. The change in angle allowed a deeper penetration, and she moaned as their slick bodies slid and rubbed together, the promise of ecstasy so close she could almost taste it. Writhing, pleading, she ground herself against Brand and at last waves of bliss surged through her body. But Brand didn't stop, just kept thrusting faster and harder, ensuring it continued on and on until finally he gasped her name, his huge body shaking as his seed gushed deep inside her. His weight was near-crushing as he collapsed on top of her, but she held him tightly, stroking his hair and crooning nonsense words. For hours they loved and rested, until dawn's uncaring rays forced themselves through the small windows. Securely wrapped in Brand's arms under the quilts, ignoring the soreness between her legs, a single tear rolled down her cheek and splashed onto his chest.

The most perfect night of her life.

And now a day of reckoning.

Chapter Six

"Brand! Stop looking at me like that. I simply cannot, er…"

He grinned at Carey's rosy cheeks, enjoying the simple pleasure of watching her perched on the end of the bed and attending to her hair, like a husband might do. "Thanks to a certain insatiable angel, I can't either. Not so much as a drop left."

"*Brandon FitzAlan.*"

"Ah, so that is how it shall be, hmm? Not even waiting until we are wed to be a scold?" he said, pulling on his boots and ducking just in time to avoid an airborne wooden comb. "Anyway, a man is well within his rights to admire his betrothed."

Betrothed.

It shouldn't feel so right when they'd only known each other for a few weeks, when they could be torn apart at any given moment, but it did. It felt right like nothing else in his world.

Fully unraveling his thoughts and emotions regarding Carey had been nigh on impossible at his home, even on the journey here. Strangely enough, it had taken succumbing to his basest needs, his guiltiest sin for all to become clear. But he had come to care deeply for this woman and would give up all he had, and then some, for her happiness. Should anyone try and harm her again, well they would swiftly learn the true meaning of hell unleashed. Arthur Linwood had cherished and protected Carey for the first twenty years of her life; Brand FitzAlan would do so for the rest. No longer would she be afraid or alone, and as his wife she would have all she desired and more.

Carey snorted and secured her plaited hair into a coil at the nape of her neck, then settled a simple hood on her head.

"There is very little to admire at the moment. I've sponged and brushed my gown twice already, but it still looks like I've been dancing in a mud puddle. And my hair… oh, what I wouldn't give for a few of Papa's soaps right now. He had a special recipe and would add different oils to scent. I especially loved the rose or lemon."

"You shall have dozens of soaps. And new gowns. I'll order so many bolts of silk and velvet that merchants will line up for miles to befriend you. Then you'll need to select fur trims and hoods, the softest linen nightgowns, stockings, petticoats, pairs of shoes, necklaces and brooches—"

Her eyes widened so far he thought they might pop out of her head. "No! That will cost a fortune."

"I am a wealthy man, Carey," he said quietly. "Very wealthy. Not many people are aware, as unlike most at court it is not something I flaunt, but between the inheritance from my grandfather, the lands I hold, and more recently, the gifts from my noble father, you shall want for nothing."

"I want you, not your bags of coins. Although I cannot wait to see your country estate and meet your mother. She sounds a wonderful lady."

"She is to me what Arthur was to you. Now, do you want anything else to eat?" he said, gesturing to the remains of their breakfast. Wanting to prolong their time alone, he'd ordered the meal of chicken broth, bread with honey, and sweet ale brought early to their chamber.

Carey's smile dimmed, the fingers of both hands twisting together as she stood. "No. Much as I wish to stay safe and warm in this room with you, we need to find the Blacksmiths as soon as possible."

"Today we will knock on every door in Guildford if we have to. Let us away, then."

Taking her arm and tucking it securely in his, Brand led her from the chamber and down the stairs toward the front of the inn. He was just about to push open the door to the large tavern area, when a meaty hand clamped on his arm.

He pivoted, preparing to grip and twist his assailant's arm until it broke, until he saw the grim face of the innkeeper.

"Yes?" said Brand quickly, his heart pounding. "Is there a problem?"

"Beg pardon, sir, but ye don't want to be goin' in there. Out back through the kitchens would be better, I'm thinkin'."

Carey gasped, and a fine mist of perspiration dampened his neck.

"Oh?"

"Maybe a quarter hour ago, a couple of rough strangers

arrived. My good wife says they are askin' a great many questions about a certain nobleman and a dark-haired doctor's daughter. Thing is though, they forgot their purses. And that doctor, he were a dab hand with elixirs for a poorly young one. So nobody here seen or heard anythin'."

"Bless you, sir," said Carey fervently.

"You be careful, mistress. And you, sir. The wife says they got a mean look about them, and she's met all types."

"Will you see to the horses?" said Brand. "Perhaps some more food for us, easily carried?"

"Aye. Oh, and by the by, the smithy I hear ye be searchin' for is three streets back and six doors down to the left. I'll tell yer servants where you've gone. *Go*."

Shoving a guinea into the innkeeper's hand, Brand hurried past the man, pulling Carey through the stifling hot kitchen and down three stone steps to a long, narrow garden. Weaving around a large pig pen, several chicken coops, and neatly-kept rows of tilled soil, he helped her over a wooden sty and onto the muddy street.

He paused, looking left and right, but they were temporarily alone, most residents of Guildford seemingly unwilling to brave the cold, rain-misted morning just yet. As an added precaution he pulled up the hood of his cloak, and Carey quickly did the same.

"Come on," he said tightly, curving an arm around her waist. "This way. We need to find the Blacksmiths before whoever was at the inn does."

"What about Lucas? And your men?"

"No one would dare touch Lucas. And my men were previously mercenaries. They know how to disappear when necessary."

Moving fast enough to put distance between them and the inn, but not so their gait would be remarked upon by anyone who happened to glance their way, they followed the innkeeper's directions to a small but well-kept smithy.

"Hello?" he called, and eventually a simply-dressed, silver-haired man came out from the back, wiping his hands on a linen cloth.

"Mornin', sir. Mistress. You must want a blacksmith right bad, to be wanderin' round the town at this time and in this weather."

"Indeed. We're very particular. We owe a great debt to a certain young Blacksmith for the service he did us, you see, and we were told by a friend his father could be found here."

Agony flashed across the man's craggy face. "Is that right?"

Abruptly Carey pushed away from him and ran up to the lean stranger. "Please, sir. This is Sir Brandon FitzAlan, and I am Catherine Linwood. My father was Doctor Arthur Linwood. I need to find the family of Robbie Blacksmith. Several days ago he saved my life, and…well…please, it is so very important, and we have little time left."

The old man stared hard at them, as though considering. Finally, he spat over his shoulder and ambled forward. "Robert Blacksmith is my name. You'd best come with me."

The cottage behind the smithy was small, but immaculately kept. Brand was forced to bend well forward to get through the low door, but Catherine had no such issue. A quick glance around the room revealed a large black kettle hanging over a roaring fire, another pot with some sort of fragrant stew bubbling away, and a hand-carved table with four chairs around it. Through a doorway to her left she spotted the end of a large bed, several colorful quilts piled high at the end.

Charmed, she smiled. "What a lovely home."

"Thankee. My wife keeps it as it should be. She would come out to greet you, but…she…she…took a draught to help her sleep. The news, you understand."

Remembered pain made her shudder.

"When I received word of my father's death," Catherine said softly, "it hurt so badly I didn't want to get out of bed. I am so sorry for your loss. And to know I was the cause of it…that is unbearable."

Robert shook his head. "No. I saw what happened on the street to my boy, and those two will meet the devil firsthand when they pass. But I am glad to see you hale and hearty, Mistress Linwood, for I had grave fears what happened to your father and Robbie would befall you also."

"Why?" asked Brand bluntly, his folded arm stance making his shoulders seem positively mountainous.

The older man hesitated, then gestured to the table. "Take a seat and I'll tell you a short tale. Perhaps some mead to warm yer bellies?"

"That would be most kind," she said, shooting Brand a significant look. "Mead is excellent for these chilly days."

Bustling around the room, Robert poured three servings of mead then fetched a short poker. After holding it over the fire, he plunged it into each tankard to heat the liquid, filling the room with the delicious scent of honey and spices.

They sipped in appreciative silence for a few minutes.

Finally, Robert put his tankard down and clasped his hands together as if in prayer.

"Several weeks ago, a man came into my smithy needin' help with a thrown horseshoe. He was a pleasant fellow, said he was a doctor, come from London to Guildford to attend the noble folk on the hill. I was surprised, seemed a long way to call a man in winter when the weather and roads are so bad. My wife, Gwen, she's a maid up at the manor, she hadn't said anything about an illness requiring that kind of help, just that the ladies were feeling a mite poorly and wanted naught but broth and watered wine."

"The ladies are close friends to Her Majesty," said Catherine slowly. "That is why she asked Papa to travel here."

Robert frowned. "I wouldn't think so. The family were strongly for Edward, then the unfortunate Jane Grey. Been keepin' to themselves since Mary took the throne, don't hold with the Catholics, you see."

Unease prickled her skin. "Then what happened?"

"The doctor stopped by several times over the next few weeks. He admired an eating dagger I crafted and asked if he could purchase it. I said that one was spoken for, but I could make him another if he told me what he liked. Very particular he was, too. Took quite some time to finish engraving the letter 'C' on the blade. Robbie was a dab hand with wood, he carved the handle with a lily. Then we wrapped it in oiled cloth and took it up to the manor."

Brand set his tankard down. "Do you still have the dagger? C is for Catherine here."

Robert nodded and hurried from the room. When he returned, he handed her a small, ribbon-tied bundle.

Unwrapping it with shaking hands, she lifted up the

palm-sized dagger, tracing the intricate carving in the blade and wooden handle with a finger.

Tears rolled down her face.

"Oh, Papa," she whispered, so heartsick she could scarcely breathe.

"He was a good man," said Robert. "Gwen said they thought very highly of him up on the hill, too. Everyone, not just the nobles. Kind to all he was, no airs and graces. That's why we were so shocked at what happened that day."

"Tell me."

"When Robbie and me rounded the corner of the stables on the way to the house, we saw him standing there talking to two burly men in the queen's colors. Well, not talking, arguing. I thought that right strange, so I pulled my boy behind a gate...oh, Lord..."

"Go on," said Brand grimly. "I know it is a terrible thing to recollect, but we need answers if there's to be any justice for my friend, for Catherine's father, for your son."

Robert's hands clenched around his tankard. "They grabbed him. One stepped behind the doctor, securing his arms behind his back and covering his mouth. The other pulled out a knife, and stabbed him four times in the gullet — "

Clamping a hand over her mouth to muffle her screams, Catherine rocked on the chair as her vision grayed, as icy shudders shook her body. Moments later she was pulled onto Brand's lap, his arms tight like a suit of armor, her only protection from the world.

"And?" he said, one hand stroking her hair.

"So fast it happened," continued Robert, "then they let him fall to the ground while one of the guards fetched a sheet from a cart. They wrapped his body, put it on the back of the cart, then drove away like the hounds of hell were at their backs."

"But why," Catherine choked out through the boulder currently resting in her throat. "Why did they kill him? What did they argue about?"

Robert paled, and she braced herself.

"It were bad," he said, his voice barely a murmur now, as though afraid the walls had ears. "The doctor didn't come here to tend noble ladies. He was banished from court because he suspected somethin' about Queen Mary and had to cool his heels until she forgave him. But Linwood didn't heed the warning. He wrote letters in his own hand to her other doctors, and they were intercepted. The guards were tauntin' him about it."

"What were the letters about?" said Brand, his acute tension clear in both his words and body. "King Phillip? Perhaps he is not the father of her child? Or the heir itself?"

"Linwood believed there ain't no heir, that it is another false pregnancy like the first one."

Silence hung like a shroud over the table as the words sunk in, but somehow the sounds of the room seemed much louder than before, the beating of Brand's heart against her ear, the crackle and spit of the fire, even the bubbling stew.

"If that is true," said Brand, and even he had lowered his voice now, "Queen Mary will be humiliated. Far worse this time. Her Spaniard has long sailed, and she is very old for childbearing. She knows it, the court knows it, and you can be damned sure every Protestant both in the country and beyond our shores knows it. This could end her reign."

Catherine sucked in a harsh breath. "The country will be torn apart again. The only direct English successor to the throne is…"

Elizabeth.

B rand could scarcely breathe.

Several times in his life he'd felt fear like this, the dark, suffocating kind that slithered and gripped relentlessly and rendered a body near-useless. As a child, hiding in ditches to avoid hurled rocks. As a too-pretty lad, cornered in taverns by noble drunks. As a man, diving into a frigid lake to find his missing wife, and lastly, on his knees next to his mother's sickbed, ordering her not to die.

They had to get away from Guildford. Immediately. Not for a moment, not in his wildest imaginings, had he considered that Arthur's secret could be this explosive. The only way he and Carey stood a chance at survival was to flee to France or perhaps one of the Low Countries. In England they would be hunted down and killed with nary a second glance, along with anyone who gave them aid.

"We must go, Robert," he said abruptly, and Carey scrambled from his lap. "Before anyone knows we were here and punishes you or your wife for it."

Their host nodded and got to his feet. "Get as far away as possible. These are dark times, Sir Brandon. If someone so close and loyal to the queen's majesty as the doctor could be murdered, no one else's life is worth a farthing. For the bloodstained Tudor throne, they'll do to you and Mistress Catherine what they did to my boy. They'll do it to anyone."

Quickly delving into his cloak pocket, Brand curled two gold sovereigns into his fingers, and when he shook Robert's hand in farewell, discreetly passed them on. The older man gaped at him, visibly shocked at the hefty sum and about to protest, but he gave a tiny shake of his head. Thanks to the Blacksmith family, Carey lived. Not only that, in the eating dagger she held a reminder of Arthur to cherish.

Opening the cottage door, Brand looked left and right, but thankfully there was no one nearby. They had probably already tarried too long and the weather had improved, the mist lifting slightly, and weak rays of sunshine attempting to burst through the morning gloom. Taking Carey's clammy hand in his, they made their way along a narrow gravel path behind the smithy and toward the adjacent street.

"Where will we go, Brand?" she asked in a hushed tone, her face starkly pale. "The coast?"

"Yes, that is what I am thinking. London is out of the question, so the next best option would be Portsmouth. Ships come and go from there all the time, if we are discreet and careful we should be able to gain passage aboard some sort of vessel to France."

"For good?"

"No, sweet," he said, rubbing a thumb over her knuckles. "Just a temporary exile, I'm sure." Well, at least he hoped it would be temporary. Thousands of Protestants had fled England to wait for better times, they could easily do the same. The queen would have to make an announcement eventually, either abdicate to Elizabeth, or perhaps even nominate a distant Catholic relation like Mary, Queen of Scots or the Plantagenet Cardinal Reginald Pole as her heir. All they had to do was stay alive and uncaptured till then.

Carey pulled her cloak hood up over her head.

"I'm g-glad we had a hearty breakfast. And that mead. It

will make the journey to Portsmouth more bearable."

Just for a moment, he halted, cupped her cheek and kissed her fiercely.

"My brave darling. Once we get my horse, we'll be fine. The saddlebags still have the canvas sheets and pegs in them to make another tent, plus our friend the innkeeper promised to pack food for us."

"Let us hurry, then. I do not wish to stay in Guildford a minute longer."

They walked in silence the rest of the way back to the inn. More and more people were in their gardens now, seeing to animals, beating carpets and airing sheets while the weather held, and he didn't want to risk anyone overhearing something damning.

Scrambling again over the sty, they crossed the inn's back garden and moved toward the stables. As though he'd been watching out for them, the innkeeper dashed out the door with a cloth-wrapped parcel.

"Here, to tide ye over. Your horse is ready for a gallop, I hope. My eldest told me he has seen soldiers in the town square, for the love of God, take the south road and do not stop for anyone."

"Thank you," said Carey, smiling warmly at the man. "We'll not forget your kindness."

Brand sprinted into the darkened stables, blinking and rubbing his eyes to adjust them to the poor light. Shoving the food parcel into a saddlebag, he swiftly checked his mount's hooves, flanks, and bridle, but the inn's stable boy had done a thorough job. Relieved, he clicked his tongue, firmly leading the horse back out into the yard.

And froze.

The innkeeper lay inert near the steps to his kitchen, a trickle of blood sliding down his temple. Carey dangled limply a foot off the ground in a scarlet-clad soldier's brutal grasp, a huge hand clamped over her mouth, while five other soldiers stood in a semi circle, blocking the only way to freedom.

"As I live and breathe, Sir Brandon FitzAlan," said the man who held Carey. "Haven't you had us all on a wild goose chase? But it is time to return to London now. There are noble folk who wish to speak to you urgently."

Brand's fists clenched. "Put her down."

"Here, now. That's not a very civil tone!"

"Immediately."

The soldier spat sideways. "Or what?"

"Or I will kill you. Slowly."

"Ha! The woman would be dead afore you got close. Be a shame, really. Since we saw the drawing of her, we been looking forward to spreading the thighs of such a plump and pretty handful. All of us," the man finished with a gruesome, gap-toothed smile as he palmed one of Carey's breasts and squeezed hard.

Black fury like he'd never known took over, and Brand flew at him. Wrenching Carey out of his filthy grasp, he wrestled the man to the ground and slammed a closed fist over and over into his face, then made him squeal as he stabbed a short dagger deep into his side.

Unfortunately that was all he managed, as all bar one of the other soldiers leapt into the fray and dragged him off their fallen friend, the other attempting to grab Carey and secure her flailing fists behind her back.

"Enough," snapped an older man, probably their captain,

shooting a disgusted look at them all. "His Grace of Norfolk's orders on behalf of the queen's majesty were clear. Sir Brandon and Mistress Linwood are to be taken back to London and examined thoroughly by the council for the grievous crimes they have committed. A cart is at the ready, we need to leave at once, not tarry here indulging in lewd talk or blood sports."

Brand struggled violently in the soldiers' grasp, rage still surging through his body, but they held firm.

"We have committed no crimes," he growled. "Whatever the charges the damned council have decreed, they are false and you all know it."

The captain shrugged, his face expressionless. "Orders are orders. I'd prefer the cooperation of yourself and the woman, but should you choose to remain defiant, I will be forced to take certain measures to ensure your obedience."

"No!" screamed Carey. "He has done nothing wrong. It is me they want. Let him go."

"Unfortunately, mistress, Norfolk requires you both, so the pair of you will be traveling to London this day. Whether hale and hearty or broken is your choice."

The polite yet merciless words caused icy chills to dance along Brand's spine. There were a great many brainless thugs in Mary's army, but the captain was not one of them. He would follow his orders to the letter, using whatever brutal means of torture necessary.

And Brandon FitzAlan, like a lovesick fool, had already shown his one true weakness. Carey. Not for a moment could he bear to see his betrothed whipped, in stocks, or worse.

Uttering a foul curse, he shook off the soldiers' loosened grasp and held out his wrists in a gesture of surrender.

"Very well. To London."

Chapter Seven

"Make way! Make way for the godless traitor filth!" Gritting his teeth at the bellowed words, Brand turned his head just in time to lessen the impact of yet another rotten vegetable. For the endless journey from Guildford to London, he and Carey had been bundled into a cart with thick iron bars. That, at least, offered some protection. But as soon as they entered the city proper, they had been hauled out, wrists bound tightly behind their backs, and forced to trudge the streets with cold, cramped limbs. They looked like beggars in their dirty, wrinkled clothing, while this particularly sadistic guard constantly announced their newly acquired status.

The people of London responded as they always did. Some silently pitying, others turning away in relief it wasn't them, and a third group who laughed, jeered and threw waste at the fall of a former royal favorite, and the black sheep of a very powerful family.

"Whip the devil's servant and his whore!"
"Not so high and mighty now, are ye?"
"Guilty. Cut off both their heads!"

He thought he'd be immune to the insults. That life as a bastard and Therese's death had long ago armored him against casually cruel strangers possessing no facts yet instantly passing judgment and pronouncing guilt. But Carey's tearful bewilderment and cries of fright and pain as she'd been taunted, spat on, and hit with all manner of foul things brought back the crushing shame, anger, and despair at the injustice of punishment for a crime not committed.

Yet even humbled as he was, the fierce protectiveness he felt toward her remained steadfast, the urge to sign his own death warrant by attacking the guards and those crowding the streets for causing her pain overwhelming. Carey saw something in him that no one else did. For once not his family name and connections, the more prominent position at court it could offer. Nor his inherited and accumulated wealth, the opportunity of a minor title or fine London home.

Just him.

How or why, he didn't know, but in offering him everything, believing in him, she in turn had made him believe.

An unholy cry yanked him back to the present."

Repent, sinners. Repent or burn!" screeched a young mother to his right, before a cold, pulpy mess hit the back of his head and sprayed fetid juice onto his neck and down his doublet collar.

By all the saints, he hated this city.

"Brand."

He turned his head at Carey's soft cry, just in time to see two leering lads take aim at her breasts with an armful of overripe tomatoes. Stepping to his left, he pivoted in front of her and deflected them with his back. He already carried the sweet scents of blood, grime, and various kitchen scraps, what were a few more servings of unwanted food?

"You know," he said conversationally, walking backward as though he did it every day of the week, "if Lucas were here, he'd be cursing the ungodliness of vegetables and how unpleasant they were to eat and wear. And I'd be forced to agree with him. So I am most relieved he was ordered home to cool his heels in Cornwall."

She stared at him for a long moment, then lifted her chin, squared her shoulders and attempted a smile. "I...I don't know. Sure I read in one of Papa's books the softer the pulp, the better for one's skin—"

"Oi! Back in formation, you!" barked a guard to their side.

So proud of Carey's spirit, Brand ignored the red-cheeked man entirely and bent down, brushing her cheek with a kiss. "Indeed."

"By the by, I know you miss him."

"Lucas? Don't be ridiculous. Tis a miracle the boy has made it to fourteen. Rafe and Annabelle de Vere must be saints, or consume enough wine to float a warship."

"Ha. Admit it, you wish for brave, amusing, troublemaking sons just like him. Like you were, I imagine."

"Sons perhaps, not sure about daughters though. I'd be driven to drink, no, far worse—driven to attend church as soon as you birthed them. Imagine the mayhem a mob of ebony-curled, sapphire-eyed FitzAlans might create—"

A heavy blow made his ears ring, and he stumbled for a few steps before regaining his balance. Probably a good thing, because he was getting far ahead of himself. Yes, she had miraculously agreed to his entirely unromantic proposal in the heat of passion, but there was still so much she didn't know about him. His father Arundel. The dark secrets of his first marriage to Therese. How deeply his anti-Catholic sentiment ran. Even if by some miracle the queen called a halt to this evil and freed them, Carey could well still turn her back on him when she discovered all the ugly truths.

Flexing his throbbing jaw, he looked steadily at Sergeant Red-cheeks. The guard sat straighter in his saddle, glaring back at him with beady ferret eyes. "I said back in formation, FitzAlan. It is less than a mile to the palace, you godless sinner. You should both be thinkin' of final confession, not laughin'. Reckon a taste of the rack might help. Sure they'd love you to visit…aw, now don't fret, mistress. Her Majesty might be merciful and send you straight to the block or pyre, being as you were a favorite for so long."

"Or," said Brand, baring his teeth in a parody of a smile, "we'll both be found innocent of all charges, released immediately, and given the freedom to find those who wronged us for a slow, messy vengeance. You've heard about me…haven't you?"

The guard made a snarling sound and deliberately spat on the toe of Brand's boot, but a moment later he pulled hard on the reins and retreated several feet.

"Brand," Carey whispered shakily after several minutes, sidling a step closer to him. "Are you hurt?"

"No," he replied, forcing a reassuring smile. "Just in desperate need of one of my betrothed's special sponge baths."

She blushed scarlet, and his smile widened to a genuine grin. But before he could say another word, a trumpet blast sounded ahead of them and all humor vanished. On the steps of St. James's Palace his father stood next to the Duke of Norfolk and the Archbishop of Canterbury. The three most powerful men in the country, all devout Catholics and loyal to the queen. All cold-eyed, cold-hearted and unsmiling.

Norfolk stepped forward, a roll of crisp parchment open in his hands.

"Sir Brandon FitzAlan, Mistress Catherine Linwood, you stand accused of high treason, blasphemy, heresy, witchcraft, and fornication. On behalf of her most gracious majesty Queen Mary, it is the desire of the council to hear this matter personally and pass judgment upon it. Due to the nature of the charges, it is also the desire of the council to begin with all haste. Therefore, your trial shall commence at noon, three days hence. Guards, escort them to the dungeon."

"No," Carey cried, frantically trying to twist out of the guards' hold as they began to roughly haul her away. "Brand. Brand!"

He ran several steps before his back arched and legs buckled under the brutal strike of wooden staffs, the agonizing burn of the heavy blows a sickening contrast to the chills roiling his gut. Once again in his wretched life, he was reduced to utter powerlessness by the whims and desires of noble-blooded Catholics.

There would be no justice here. Mary wanted them both dead.

They would take her secrets to the grave.

Three days.

Three endless days she had spent confined to this

shadowed, damp, sparsely furnished chamber in a forgotten corner of St. James's Palace, her only indication of time passing a small ledged window that allowed a few weak rays when the sun rose to its highest point in the sky. Three days of forced contemplation, as she was permitted no books, quill and parchment, embroidery, or even rosary beads for solace.

Three days of near-silence. The silver-haired maid who delivered trays of bread, fruit, and a bowl of thin broth twice daily and emptied her chamber pot never spoke a word. Another who left a change of clean clothing—linen chemise and petticoat, plain white cloth hood, and gray wool gown—refused to meet her gaze. In fact the only person she'd conversed with since the start of her imprisonment was a wizened old man named Parsons who visited each morning, and when not dozing, called himself her legal representative.

But by far the worst punishment, three days of not seeing Brand. Not hearing his voice, touching him, feeling the warmth and strength of his arms around her. Was he nearby? Badly injured from his beating? Longing for her the way she did him?

He cared for her. Perhaps he might not have said the words, but so many times he had shown her in deeds, putting his own life at risk for her again and again. Yet now that they were both arrested and imprisoned, the stakes were so much higher. What if Brand had been broken on the rack and forced to a devil's bargain—his life entirely restored in exchange for a damning witness?

Certain she'd never be warm again, Catherine huddled under a thin blanket on the narrow pallet-bed, her tears long run dry. Abruptly the clank and grind of a lock needing oil echoed through the chamber, and the heavy oak door scraped open to reveal Master Parsons and two armed soldiers.

"It is…it is time?" she croaked through the boulder lodged in her throat.

"Aye, mistress. You must come with us to face the council and answer the charges against you."

Bracing one hand on the cold stone wall, she climbed off the unsteady pallet and smoothed her gown. "Yes, sir. I am ready."

Such was the size of St. James's Palace, they rounded many corners and marched countless hallways, and still she could not see so much as a familiar tapestry. Eventually they reached a set of five wide steps set under a great archway—the entrance to what looked like a disused great hall.

Weapons thumped on the floor.

"Mistress Catherine Linwood!"

It was a familiar call, but today there were no respectful bows or cheerful hails. She faltered, until a firm shove to the back forced her through the door of the room deemed fit to be her and Brand's place of judgment. Shockingly, a sea of people sat on cushioned chairs either side of a narrow aisle. All chatter ceased, only emphasizing the drag and clatter of her ill-fitting shoes on the polished wooden floor, the wheezing breaths from Master Parsons shuffling behind her.

A clerk darted forward and gestured for her to sit atop a stool resting on a raised platform, the square surrounded by a thin metal railing. Taking several deep breaths, she lifted her head and faced the council. Today just five of the extraordinarily powerful men would decide her fate: Thomas Howard, Duke of Norfolk; Henry FitzAlan, Earl of

Arundel; Reginald Pole, Archbishop of Canterbury; Francis Talbot, Earl of Shrewsbury; and Thomas Percy, Earl of Northumberland.

Norfolk stood. Today he wasn't Jane's brother, the man who had distributed coins for hair ribbons and taught them cards, but an ice-cold, utterly aloof stranger looking every inch England's premier nobleman.

"Please state your name for the court, madam."

"Catherine Mary Linwood. Daughter of the late Arthur Linwood, physician."

"You know why you are here?"

"Yes, your grace. To answer charges against me."

"High treason," he snapped, his voice the crack of a whip. "Heresy. Witchcraft. Fornication. The fifth charge of blasphemy has already been found wanting and dismissed. So without further ado, let the first witnesses be brought in to the charge of witchcraft."

Leaning forward, Catherine rested white-knuckled hands on the railing as she heard from a trio of respectable women the long and harrowing tale of a black-haired witch who shamelessly used flowers to lure an innocent young man to his doom. How she'd stood between him and two brave guards who might save him, then cast a spell causing him to fly from the footpath to the middle of the road and perish under a cart.

Gasps rolled like thunder through the hall.

"Your reply, Master Parsons?" barked Norfolk, silencing the din.

Across the aisle from her, the lawyer rose to his feet and coughed. "Good women, are you sure it was Mistress Linwood you saw on that sad day?"

"Yes," they replied as one.

"Oh," he said and sat down.

She stared. *Oh?* That was all the old man could say to such a twisted version of the truth?

"Excuse me, your grace," she began, addressing Norfolk. "I must—"

"There is no must in this court, Mistress Linwood. Your chance to speak will come later in proceedings. Now let us hear the next witness, to the charge of heresy and high treason."

The sound of heels clicking on the wooden floor and the rustle of heavy silk were unbearably loud in the eerie quiet, and chills slithered down her spine at who might now seek to damn her.

Master Parsons stood again. "Your name, madam?"

The woman turned.

"Lady Jane Howard," said Jane, settling herself on a high-backed chair.

Pressing a fist to her mouth to muffle a scream of denial, Catherine stared in shock at her friend. It was all becoming clearer now, Jane's disappearance from court and lack of any contact after Papa's death. When had she been told? Did she choose to do this or was she a witness by force? Could there be a tiny chance Jane might offer testimony to save her?

"Lady Jane," said Master Parsons gently. "You claim witness to acts of heresy and high treason by Mistress Linwood?"

"I do. It is my great shame I once called her friend, but she hid her sinful heart well for a time. Until the day her father died."

Agony threatened to tear her apart. The friend she had loved like a sister was about to calmly destroy her?

"Oh, Jane," she whimpered through bloodless lips. "Please, please no…"

"What happened that day, my lady?" said Master Parsons.

"We were on our way to an audience with Her Majesty. We spoke of the impending blessed event. But Catherine… Mistress Linwood that is, forcibly diverted the conversation to a time…when something occurred that caused great sadness to our beloved queen. Then she expressed the deepest sympathies toward the Lady Elizabeth. Despite weak protests she was a good and loyal Catholic, I could only conclude, sir, that Mistress Linwood wished death to God's anointed sovereign and her unborn child, and the throne be snatched by Lutherans."

The hall erupted in a deafening chorus of furious shouts, foot stomping, jeers and threats. Tears flowing freely down her face, Catherine wrapped her arms around herself and rocked during the several minutes of Norfolk banging his gavel to restore order.

"Do you have anything final to add, Lady Jane?" asked Master Parsons.

"Indeed," said Jane sharply, rising to her feet. "God save and bless Queen Mary!"

Several hundred voices echoed the sentiment as she departed, over and over until Norfolk banged the gavel again.

"Silence in the court," he said irritably, "or I will clear it. We have one final witness today, to the charge of fornication. Bring in…Sir Brandon FitzAlan."

G od rot the hypocrites in this hall.

As he leisurely made his way to the front, Brand kept his hands by his sides, his face impassive. Surrounded by sinners, on the council and not, every second man guilty of the crimes he'd been accused of. Fornication? Each day and then some. Heresy? Should the queen perish and Elizabeth succeed, thousands would recant faster than they blinked. Witchcraft? Treason? Those crimes entailed whatever those on high said they did. Yesterday's healers and favorites were today's witches and traitors, as everyone knew.

The five councilmen, Norfolk, Arundel, Shrewsbury, Northumberland, and Pole, watched him like hawks, but not by so much as a twitch of the brow or lagging footfall did he reveal the burning agony of each step thanks to the prolonged punishment in front of the palace. They would see an unafraid, hale and hearty man, not one suffering a mess of welts, cuts, and black and purple-streaked bruising.

He allowed himself one long look at Carey as he settled into a chair, drinking in the sight of her like a parched man at a stream, willing her to lift her gaze from the floor. Finally she did, and the streaks of tears, the hollow despair there was nearly his undoing.

Almost imperceptibly, he inclined his head.

Be strong, sweetheart. We shall win through this. Somehow.

His lawyer, a slippery, buck-toothed man named Clements, bowed to the councilmen. "If I might begin, your grace, Archbishop, my lords?"

With the panel's permission, Clements turned back to him.

"Please confirm your name for the court."

"Sir Brandon FitzAlan."

"Son of?"

Brand looked directly at Arundel. "No one of note."

"Er…very well. Let us—"

"One moment," said Norfolk, holding up a hand. "Today, Sir Brandon, you are not the accused, but an important witness to the unspeakable crimes of one Mistress Catherine Linwood. This is your opportunity to provide a full and frank disclosure of your observations and clarify certain other matters. Any assistance will be favorably taken into account by this court, alongside expression of remorse, when judging your own misdeeds."

Shock and rage surged through his veins at the honey-phrased invitation to betrayal.

Hurl Carey to the wolves and walk free.

The offer could only mean the duke knew Arundel was father to his key witness. Then again, Norfolk had briefly been Arundel's son-in-law, so he probably knew all the family skeletons.

"I shall keep that in mind, your grace," Brand said without inflection.

"Excellent. Pray continue, Master Clements."

The lawyer bowed. "Sir Brandon, would you tell the court how you met Mistress Linwood?"

"When I paid my respects at Arthur Linwood's funeral. The doctor and I were fast friends prior to his most untimely passing."

"So at a time of sacred mourning she lured you into temptation?"

"No. Mistress Linwood was an innocent, respectable, learned woman in need of a friend. And her father saved my mother's life. I *offered* my assistance in any way it might be required."

"And what was the boon she asked of you?"

"To find out the actual cause of her father's death—"

Norfolk banged his gavel. "Arthur Linwood passed of a fever. Master Clements, your witness is to clarify a charge of fornication, please phrase your questions more appropriately."

"Beg pardon, your grace," said Clements, paling. "Sir Brandon, on the day of March twenty-fifth when Mistress Linwood caused the death of that poor young man and escaped her guards, did she coerce you into taking her to safety?"

"She caused no deaths. And no, I chose to assist her."

"Did she bribe you with use of her body in exchange for the protection?"

"No, she did not."

"I see. When you both fled to Guildford with Master Lucas de Vere and three servants, had she coerced or bribed you to do so?"

"No, she did not."

"But whilst in that town, at an inn, you shared a room with Mistress Linwood. Did you engage in carnal relations with her outside the holy bonds of matrimony?"

Brand hesitated. "I…"

"Come now. The court can easily order an examination of Mistress Linwood to establish her virginity or lack thereof."

Nausea roiled his gut at the thought, and he gritted his teeth. "Yes, we engaged in carnal relations."

Clements beamed, his relief palpable at a positive answer. "Pray continue. Did Mistress Linwood instigate the carnal relations?"

As one, every man in the room leaned in like a pack of starving hounds to a fox. He ignored them all and instead looked at Carey, meeting and holding her gaze, attempting to convey a silent promise of care and loyalty.

"You insult me, sir. I am a man of much experience and Mistress Linwood an untouched virgin. Of course it was not her who instigated."

"So you claimed her maidenhead at that inn?"

"Yes. I am entirely at fault. Mistress Linwood is a clever, amusing, kind, and beautiful woman who I had developed strong feelings for, and when an opportunity arose to indulge my base desires, I took it. Any punishment for this crime is mine and mine alone to bear. If a whipping is called for, then let me be whipped at once and be done."

He glanced again at Carey, and this time she sat straighter on the stool, a hint of color at her cheeks and her gaze steady. In one deliberate movement, she touched two fingers to her lips, then her heart. The room erupted in noise at the gesture, and Norfolk nearly hammered a hole in his wooden desk as he attempted to bring the hall under control.

Quickly the duke conferred in whispers with the other members of the panel, in what looked to be a rather heated discussion.

"Thank you, Sir Brandon," Norfolk said coldly, several minutes later, "but this court will decide the recipients of punishment and what that punishment will be, not you. As a matter of fact, we the council find your comments startling and clear evidence of an unreasonably fatigued mind. After rest and refreshment, you will no doubt answer with much improved thought and logic. We will adjourn and recommence on the morrow."

Instantly he knew what must be said. Yes, it was the worst possible time for honesty. He was in a corrupt court with his freedom, his possessions, and if his own trial proceeded like this, potentially his very life on the line, but he was so bloody weary of lies and pretence. Of being a powerless pawn in the games of noblemen.

Damned if he would play for another moment.

"With all due respect, your grace," he said loudly enough for the entire hall to hear him, "my ardent admiration, care, and support for Mistress Linwood will not change. Not tomorrow, or any other day. So make your ruling and let us be done with this charade."

Norfolk's eyes bulged. "Then you leave us no choice but to find you guilty of fornication. With respect to the other charges, you will be taken to the Tower and privately examined further."

"No," said Carey hoarsely, leaping off her stool and gripping the railing as she leaned forward. "No, no, no! He spoke untruth. It wasn't him, t'was me on the street, at his home and at the inn. I—"

"Silence!" roared Norfolk. "Judgment is passed. And you, madam, shall be heard in the morning then learn your own fate. Guards, remove the prisoners."

In a moment of clumsily exquisite timing, both sets of guards tried to march them down the middle aisle first. Within a tangle of bodies, he managed to elbow two men out of the way, and crush Carey's lips with his, one hard, brutal, final kiss of farewell.

Mary and her nobles had won.

It was over.

Chapter Eight

Brand had announced publicly he cared for and supported her. Which made him the most wonderful — and unwise — man in England.

Hugging her arms around herself, Catherine paced the short length of her palace prison chamber. The night was pitch-black and the moon barely a sliver of crescent in the sky, but she couldn't sleep. Not with these fierce emotions pounding her body and soul like battering rams. Did she laugh with the sheer joy of loving and being cared for in return, the perfection of their night together, when she learned the blissful secrets of passion? Or sob her heart out knowing it would never happen again, indeed that Brand was lost to her forever and tonight might well be her last in the mortal realm?

She groaned aloud and dropped to her knees. The stone floor scraped through the thin wool gown, but prayer was prayer, even without the familiar comfort of polished wooden rosary beads to twist through her fingers.

"Blessed Virgin, I beseech thee, hear my prayer in this, my darkest hour—"

Terror silenced her as the creak and grind of her chamber door being slowly unlocked echoed through the tiny space. No! It wasn't time. She had until morning. Unless Brand had faltered under further torture and they now possessed enough information to declare her guilty? Was she, like her father, to be denied a full trial, denied even a formal execution and killed in secret?

"Wh-who goes th-there?" she croaked.

The door opened, and a well-dressed man stepped into the room.

"Mistress Linwood. I apologize for the hour, but I must speak with you in all haste."

Shock dropped her jaw, but somehow she managed to form words and force them past a desert-dry tongue. "My Lord Arundel. Come in. Do you wish to sit?"

"Yes. No. Damnation, this is a sorry business," the earl snapped, adjusting several glittering gems on his fingers and rubbing his chin in quick succession. "Don't know what your father was thinking, creating such a tall tale as Her Majesty not truly expecting a child. The horror of it. The disgrace! Do you know what that would do to the queen if that news spread? What it would do to England? When you know the assertion is false?"

"I do," said Catherine softly. "It would be dangerous and devastating for the realm, and for every faithful Catholic. But never shall I know why my father said such a terrible thing, when he was cut down in cold blood, far from home and far from me."

Arundel looked away. "Well. You think you are the only one to lose a loved one suddenly? These two years past I watched the burial of my son and daughter. Younger than you! Now I have but one child, a daughter, remaining."

She stared at the man for the longest time. Never had she been so close to the exalted earl before, and now she was, a truth was suddenly so very clear.

"Oh really?" she whispered fiercely, fury at how this man had treated her beloved making her bolder than she'd ever been. "Just the one daughter?"

He cursed viciously. "If you understand that, then perhaps you understand why I come here. Brandon is foolish and headstrong, just like his mother. He seeks to battle those on the council, battle the queen, because he had you and wrong-headedly thinks it might be something more than simple lust. Should my son be racked for that sin? Should he die for it?"

Misery weighed on her shoulders like a load of rocks. "No. I couldn't bear it."

"Do you care for him?"

"I love him," Catherine said starkly.

"Then I beg you, let him go."

"Let him go? You are right, he is headstrong, and perhaps foolish to care for an orphaned nobody like me. But thanks to his mother and grandfather and uncle he is a man worthy of great respect. Brave and strong, willing to fight for justice and protect those weaker than him. I love his warmth. His kindness. The way he curses. The way he kisses. The way he grumbles at Lucas even as he teaches him how to be the best of men. Yes, my lord, I love your son Brand, and you ask me to turn my back as if he were nothing? As you did his whole life?"

Arundel spluttered. "You go too far, girl. I gained him what he has, a house, knighthood, fortune, position at court."

"All pale compared to a father's open pride and affection. You deny your son at every turn, call him cousin when he is not."

"I cannot claim him now. Not when I have my young grandson's future to consider. The scandal…"

Puzzled, she frowned. "Old King Henry acknowledged his natural son. Men do all the time. Tis the talk of a week then forgotten."

"Indeed, but Henry Fitzroy did not murder his wife."

Catherine choked on a breath, like she'd been pummeled in the stomach.

"Wh-what?"

An expression flashed across the earl's face, too swift for her to decipher.

"I didn't want to have to say this. The shame is a great burden to bear. But you know Brandon was married?"

"Yes, to Therese Fairfax."

"I blame myself. Therese was too young, but Brandon so…so…*desperately* in love with her, he begged me to help him win her hand. What could I do? It was the first time he'd come to me for assistance, apart from securing your father's services for Susanna, of course. So they were wed, and all was well for a while."

"And th-then?" she asked shakily.

"Brandon is very possessive. He…accused Therese of seeing other men, even that the babe she carried wasn't his, and they had many terrible fights. Until one night, he drank far too much then dragged her out to the lake behind their country home and drowned her."

"I cannot believe that," she said dizzily, her head whirling as she remembered snatches of court conversations, the heaviness surrounding Therese Fairfax's sudden death. "Brand would never…there would have been a trial…he wishes to wed me…"

"No! I mean…all the witnesses disappeared, but the whispers, they will swirl forever. My dear, again, I beg you. Not just for his sake, or mine, but your own. Deny him. Tell him you don't love or want to marry him, that it was a passing fancy, nothing more."

Numb anguish settled like a suffocating cloak. Brand himself had warned her he was darkness and danger, although she'd never imagined his past could include such a grave sin. And yet…even guilty, even if a dead woman forever held his heart, life without him still stretched ahead of her chasm, gray and equally empty.

"What do you wish me to do?" she said dully.

"If you are gone, he will enjoy court as he should. Marry a suitable lady, become a father, be welcomed at every hearth and free from the taint of treason. And you shall live."

"How?"

"There is a ship departing for France in a few hours. I will give you passage, enough money to begin a new life far from here as a boon to my son. Also because I know what it means to be falsely accused, arrested and imprisoned, and do not wish that on any soul, least of all a true Catholic and good servant of the queen. Let me help you."

Catherine shuddered, her heart breaking.

"I must pen him a letter."

Arundel's shoulders sagged. "No, he wouldn't believe that. Come with me now, say your farewells, and you'll be safe from him, from the queen and council. I swear it on my life."

Cold enveloped her, and a single tear slid down her cheek, but she nodded slowly.

"Very well."

"FitzAlan. Get up, wretch."

The swift boot to the shin would probably result in another bruise, but he was beyond caring. Since the moment he'd left the court he'd been in this tiny windowless chamber, unfurnished save a rickety wooden chair, while several senior clerks took turns questioning him on every aspect of the past few weeks. They seemed to believe taunting him, denying him food and sleep, and pouring freezing water over his head when he didn't answer fast enough would gain what they wanted.

Ha. These men could try forever, even rack him to within an inch of his life, and he still wouldn't confess to a crime he hadn't committed. Nor would he implicate Carey. Fatigue and pain were nothing compared to the memory of their last kiss, her signal in the courtroom that he held a place in her heart. That sustained him now. Would have to.

"FitzAlan!"

Brand blinked and smiled pleasantly at the scowling, pock-faced guard. "You bellowed?"

"I said get up. Yer bein' moved."

"Excellent. The view from this chamber is most sub-standard."

He rose to his feet and for one awful moment thought his shaky legs would buckle under him. But at last they steadied, and he stretched to full height, flexing muscles that burned from misuse.

"Come along then," the guard said, gripping his upper arm. "And don't give me no trouble, or you'll be gettin' the thrashin' those clerks were too soft-bellied to give."

It felt like they trudged the silent hallways of St. James's Palace for hours, and trickles of perspiration soon bathed his temples as he focused on remaining upright. But instead of leaving for a barge to Traitor's Gate, they continued on to a section of the palace where the carpets were richer and thicker, the tapestries newer and more colorful.

He frowned. "Are you lost? This won't get me to the Tower."

The guard ignored him, abruptly halting in front of a nondescript, partially open door. A moment later he was shoved through it, the door swiftly being closed and locked behind him.

Alone in the candlelit space, Brand rubbed his eyes as a strange, heavy scent enveloped him. *Incense.* He was in the chapel antechamber? Why the hell would he be brought here?

Light footsteps sounded behind him and he spun, the ill-thought movement nearly sending him crashing to the floor. God's blood, now he was hallucinating, for an angel stood before him. A shockingly pale, sapphire-eyed angel only missing her wings.

"Carey," he said hoarsely, one hand reaching out for her, but now his legs ceased to function and he staggered, bumping into a cloth-covered side table. Yet it didn't matter, for a moment later she hurled herself into his arms, buried her face against his chest and dampened the collar of his filthy doublet with tears. "Brand…"

"What are you doing here?" he said, tangling his fingers in her unbound hair, taking her lips in a hard, lingering kiss. "What am I doing here? How did you arrange it?"

She pulled back slightly, one hand sliding up to trace his forehead, jaw and lips. "I-I have c-come to…"

"Come to what, sweetheart?" he said. Carey was far too pale, too tense, and the agonized misery in her eyes made his gut churn in trepidation. "Tell me."

"Mistress Linwood has come to make her farewells," said a crisp, familiar voice as Arundel stepped out of the shadows. "After much discussion, she accepted my offer of passage to France and funds for a new life there. She knows there is nothing left for her in England but the queen's wrath and a dishonorable death. For that is the only decision the council can and will come to."

Acute unease swirled, and he stared hard at his father. "After much discussion? What could the Earl of Arundel possibly have to privately discuss with a condemned prisoner, my lord?"

"She guessed, Brandon. About our…true relationship."

"Even now, you cannot say the words. But how is that information worthy of such a generous boon as freedom?"

"I told her the rest. About—"

"He told me all about Therese and her death," said Carey, cupping his face in her delicate hands. "And despite that, I lo—"

"Despite…what?" he replied, gently removing her hands from his face and turning to his father. "Precisely which version of the story did you share with my betrothed?"

Arundel hesitated, a distinctly hunted expression appearing on his face. "The truth, of course."

Icy rage surged through his veins, and he stormed toward the earl. "Liar."

"Brand! No!" said Carey behind him, but his fist had already curled with the force of thirty years of anger and ploughed into Arundel's face, sending an arc of bright red blood spraying across the antechamber wall.

"Damnation, boy," Arundel hissed, yanking a handkerchief from his cloak pocket to stem the flow. "You broke my nose."

"I doubt that. The FitzAlan nose is rather robust. But a few more blows should do the trick."

"All right! All right. Perhaps I told the supposed story. But no one believes your version, Brandon. And there are no witnesses."

"Incorrect. There were several witnesses, and they are all safe and well in a location I won't share. They know Therese never wanted to marry me, nor I her. They know she wept every day for her lost calling as a nun, how she loathed her forced marriage and the marriage bed. And they know her pregnancy tipped the hatred into madness, as she dressed herself in ancient chainmail and waded into the lake while I met with my steward…"

He paused, as the familiar grief and anger and guilt threatened to send him to his knees. "She took her own life rather than be married to me and birth my child. I knew then that my mother was wrong and all others were right. I was poison. A worthless bastard—"

"No," said Carey fiercely, yanking his arm until he faced her, taking both his hands in hers. "No you are not. You are everything I ever wanted, ever dreamed of. I love you. I cannot help loving you and will do so forever. Whatever happens, the only reason I would go to France alone is to see you safe and well, after all you did for me."

"Sweetheart, I…" he said, humbled and overcome by her words, unable to control the grin threatening to split his face in two. "…I forbid you to go to France alone. We'll go together, you and I, and make a new life."

"Together?" she repeated, an answering smile lighting up her face. "Always."

"Wretched pair," snarled Arundel. "If you refuse to be parted, then you'll both get on that damned ship immediately. If we leave now—"

"On the contrary, my lord Arundel. Neither Sir Brandon, nor Catherine will be departing this place."

The biting chill of the deep, manly voice from the direction of the chapel froze him to the bone, and all three of them dropped to one knee and bowed their heads.

The Queen of England.

Mary's walk toward them was a slow, labored shuffle, but Catherine kept her gaze resolutely on the floor. Now was not the time for bold words or actions, not when this woman held the power of life or death for them all. Even if she did want to scream and rage at the woman she'd once loved above all, for the wicked, ungodly deeds she had ordered.

"So, you meet in secret to plot," the queen continued, her voice rising. "My loyal earl, the woman I treated like a daughter, and her errant lover. In truth you're all three for my bastard half-sister, aren't you? Looking to toss us away and usurp our hard-won throne because we cannot give England what it desperately needs. We tried! We tried so hard. But we made mistakes. We were lenient toward the heretics and sinners, and God punished us. So we burned and burned to prove our faith. But it is still not enough. Our Lord has struck us down again."

Catherine frowned at the hysteria, the torment in the queen's words. What on earth was she talking about?

"*Majesty*," Arundel's horrified voice shattered the eerie silence. "Your belly…"

She couldn't help it, her head jerked up. A gasp tore from her throat.

Queen Mary's previously hugely rounded belly had near-disappeared.

"No child," Brand said softly, beside her. "Arthur was right."

"He was not right!" Mary hissed, her arms flailing wildly. "He stole our child. Our beautiful boy, the image of Phillip. Yes, stolen. Or poisoned, no, that is what happened. Arthur Linwood poisoned us. Pretended he cared for our health when all the while he plotted and schemed with his pills and fusions to ensure Elizabeth succeeded the throne. Well she won't! Never! Phillip will return to us and we shall have a child, the most perfect Catholic prince the world has ever seen. You will see! E-everyone will s-seeeeee…"

Mary crumpled to the floor, rocking in place while she buried her face in her hands and sobbed.

Closing her eyes, Catherine offered a silent prayer that she wasn't about to make the worst mistake of her life. Before she lost her nerve, before the Christian desire to forgive passed, she crawled forward and wrapped her arms around the queen's shoulders.

"Oh, Majesty," she whispered. "I am sorry for your pain."

Mary froze then burrowed against her like a small child, longing for a little affection. "It is over, Catherine. I sought to right the wrongs of my father and brother, to secure the throne forever and make England great again. But I have failed. Soon everyone will know how badly Bloody Mary failed. All because I cleansed my realm of heretics as told to. No one will remember the good, now. Only…this."

Catherine lifted her gaze to the two men. Both remained silent, watching her, but Arundel inclined his head and Brand smiled and gestured for her to continue.

"Please, madam, you need to rest," she said to Mary. "Then—"

Abruptly the queen disengaged herself from Catherine's hold and slowly got to her feet, brushing some dust from her embroidered purple robe.

"We do not," she said coolly, distantly, like the previous minutes never happened. "The daughter of Henry the Eighth and Catherine of Aragon must carry on, with head held high. There is much still to be achieved in our realm."

"And what," said Arundel, his voice shaking, "what of my *son* Brandon and Mistress Linwood?"

Mary blinked, her regard flicking from the earl to Brand and back. "Ah…side by side you can see it. But let us ask them this: did either seek to achieve or plot our death?"

"Never, Majesty," said Catherine fervently.

"Practice witchcraft?"

"No. I swear on my father's grave."

The queen flinched. "We deeply regret…that is, we did not seek…every day a ruler is forced to make unpleasant decisions. We have prayed and prayed for absolution. But that is in the past and cannot be changed, unlike your future. We accept there has been no wrongdoing save the crime of fornication. Sir Brandon!"

"Yes, Majesty?" said Brand, getting to his feet.

"You committed a sin in taking Catherine to your bed without the blessing and sanctification of the church in marriage vows. It is our understanding you accept blame for this and have been physically corrected."

"Several times, Majesty."

"Then it is our decree that you make final amends for your actions and take Catherine to wife with all haste."

Catherine's breath hitched. Was it possible? Mary pardoning them both and ordering a dream future?

Brand bowed. "As you wish."

"You are both also ordered to leave this realm, on the ship Arundel spoke of," said Mary sharply. "We shall announce your shocking midnight escape from imprisonment in due course. Do not return here, or speak of this time to anyone, on pain of death. Do you understand? We do not ever wish to be reminded of these events."

"Yes, Majesty," said Catherine, sinking into a deep curtsey.

"Good. Arundel!"

"Majesty?" said the earl, scrambling to his feet and bowing.

"Cease sniveling into that handkerchief and escort us to our chamber."

As soon as they were alone in the anteroom, Catherine ran into Brand's open arms with a small cry, clasping him so tightly he groaned.

"No!" she said, belatedly remembering. "Your back. I'm so sorry."

"Sure I'll survive. And I can think of several ways you could make it up to me."

Her cheeks burned. "Well, no one needs a bath more than you. Let us hope your father's ship contains an entire hold of lye soap."

"That scold again! At least you hold no comb to throw today."

Catherine hesitated, biting her lip. "Do...do you truly wish to wed me?"

"I must insist. For I have no chance of joy or contentment in my life without you in it. You are...dawn after the longest night."

"*Brand.*"

"Besides, I have no desire to be whipped for fornication every other day."

"Oh you!" she gasped, giggling for the first time in what felt like eternity. Until he took her hands in his and kissed each one, silencing her with the intensity of his gaze.

"Marry me, Catherine Mary Linwood. Wed me, love me, and I should be the happiest man in England...and er, France."

Bliss overwhelmed her, and she went up on her toes to brush his lips with hers.

"I will. And I do. Forever."

Epilogue

"The queen is dead. Long live the queen!"

The hoarse cry of the exhausted herald echoed through the village square, but none who heard the words were surprised. After her second false pregnancy Mary had fallen ill, and Lucas's last letter from London where he now resided with the Dudley family, indicated she'd barely left her rooms in months. Indeed, that was the reason he and Carey dared come home to England, discreetly returning aboard a merchant ship two weeks previously.

Brand glanced down at his wife, but she seemed to be accepting of the news.

"All right, Lady FitzAlan?"

She turned and smiled at him. "Yes and no. Mary did me great kindnesses and a great harm. But because of her I found you, so I do mourn her passing. And I believe, yes I do think Elizabeth will be a good queen. More tolerant of religion at least."

"Lucas is already establishing himself as a favorite of hers. I've heard it from several people, even Arundel. Quite how, I'm unsure. Especially with his ceaseless chatter and habit of name-shortening."

Carey's eyes widened in horror. "Please don't tell me he calls the new Queen of England, *Lizzie*."

His lips twitched. "Bess. Because Elizabeth is far too long a name for a fifteen year old to remember, don't you know."

"That boy!"

"I know," he said mildly, too content with life to worry further about Lucas and his leaps from one outrageous matter to the next. "But we should be getting home. Mother is coming over from the cottage with a new tapestry to show off, and naturally I wish to order supper before the roar of your growling stomach frightens the neighbors...ow."

"Oh, I'm sorry, was that your foot?" she said, very sweetly as they passed several shops and the smithy. "But it is imperative you feed me."

"Really? Why is that? You wish to drag me into yet another darkened alcove? Have mercy, my lady, I'm an old man. I need a little recovery time, at least."

"Perhaps later. I require food to ensure the child I carry is born strong and healthy."

Brand stilled, swallowing hard against a rush of powerful elation. "A baby?"

"Well, yes. When you constantly make love to your wife in alcoves and meadows, on desks and carpets, even in an actual bed, it happens. He or she will be born sometime in the spring, I think. Are you pleased?"

He leaned down and captured her lips with his, while one hand rested on her still-flat belly. "I am at once thrilled and excited and anxious."

"As am I. But my father safely delivered many babies, and I feel…I feel he will watch over me and ensure all will be well."

Nodding solemnly, he scooped Carey into his arms and turned down the beaten path to their charming red-brick manor, with its lush fields, colorful gardens, and single orchard.

A home. Love. In time, a child.

All he desired and more.

OTHER BOOKS BY NICOLA DAVIDSON

His Forbidden Lady

Acknowledgments

A special thank you and non-awkward bear hug to Jackie Ashenden for friendship and support, editor Kate Brauning for margin smiley faces and a truckload of good points, and the Ferners for the cheers and, er, helpful suggestions. You guys rock.

About the Author

Nicola Davidson worked for many years in communications and marketing as well as television and print journalism, but hasn't looked back since she decided writing wicked historical romance was infinitely more fun. When not chained to a computer she can be found ambling along one of New Zealand's beautiful beaches, cheering on the champion All Blacks rugby team, history geeking on the internet, or daydreaming. If this includes chocolate—even better!

Keep up with Nicola's news on Twitter, Facebook (Nicola Davidson – Author) or her website www.nicola-davidson.com.